Sangria
Forever

LYNN JOSEPH

BLACK MERMAID PRESS
BOOKS THAT CHALLENGE THE STATUS QUO

 Get a Free Romance Novel! 🤍

Escape to Italy with Princess Abroad, a captivating royal romance filled with love, adventure, and breathtaking scenery. Sign up for my newsletter today and claim your free copy!

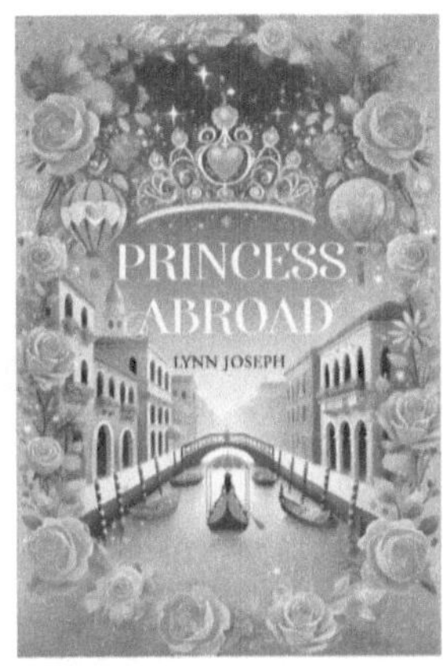

Sign up here —> https://BookHip.com/NKSQGRS

Prologue

Alone in Athens now that my sister Bridget has taken the ferry to the island of Aegina to make up with the love of her life, I call Salvador to find out what time the game is—no way I'm missing out on a fun evening with him.

Meeting him on the plane to Athens was pure chance. Going to his football game. Now, that's a plan.

"Olá, Corrine," he says in Portuguese.

His deep voice brings an instant smile to my lips.

"Bridget can't make the football game tonight. She has to go see a man about some olives."

"That doesn't sound creepy at all."

I laugh out loud. "But I'm coming. Just tell me when and where."

"I'll send a car to pick you up at seven."

"Nice."

"I can't wait to see you again."

I detect a hint of relief in his voice.

"Were you worried I wouldn't come see you play?" I tease.

"Nah!" he says too fast.

"Liar."

"A little bit. When you said Bridget wasn't coming, I thought maybe . . ."

"Well, darling, you'll have me all to yourself."

Salvador's deep chuckle shifts something inside me. My heart? No. More like my common sense.

"I'll be waiting outside the arena at the players' entrance for you."

"As you should be," I joke. "It's my first ever soccer match. Should I wear anything special?"

"Less is more as they say in America, right?" His sexy accent has me shaking my head.

He sounds exactly like the flirty bad boys I've sworn to stay away from during my year abroad. Bad boys are magnets to me. And I'm done with them.

"I meant what colors, smarty pants."

"Anything but yellow and black, please. Unless you plan on repping Athens. I'd have to seat you on the other side of the *football* stadium."

"Got it. *Football.*"

"Yeah, it's an important word on this side of the Atlantic Ocean."

"Consider me schooled, professor."

He laughs. "I wish I could see your face right now. Want to turn on your video chat?"

I pat down my long, flyaway hair that hasn't seen a comb since morning. "You'll see me soon enough. As you said, 'less is more.'"

Stop flirting with the man, it can't go anywhere.

"There's one other thing."

"Yes?"

"After the game, the team is having a party to celebrate a teammate's birthday. Would you like to go with me?"

Would I like to go to a party with this hunk? Hmmm . . . let me think.

My fingers fly to my right earlobe, rubbing vigorously. A football game is an event. He plays. I watch. But a party — that sounds like a date. Am I breaking my promise to myself already?

"You there?"

"I'm thinking." I rub my earlobe harder. "Is this like a date?"

"No."

"Whew! Okay, then."

"It's not *like* a date. It *is* a date."

"Fig!"

That deep throaty chuckle revs up my blood flow.

Say no, Corrine. It's two letters. N and O.

"Sure, I'd love to," I enthuse, rolling my eyes at my lack of willpower.

When we hang up, I sink into the sofa to evaluate the situation.

The old Corrine wouldn't hesitate to date this hunky football-playing bad boy. Who she met yesterday. On an airplane!

The new Corrine wants intellectuals, not jocks. She wants good guys who want to stay awhile, not 'here today, gone tomorrow' men.

And Salvador Torres is not the 'stay awhile' type. I've seen the way women (and men) fawn all over him. Like he's Gerard Butler in the movie *300* (if we're doing Greek references.)

How good of a football player is he anyway to warrant lines of autograph seekers and a paparazzi following?

I type the name 'Salvador Torres' into Google and lean back on the sofa cushions to wait. I tap my nails on my phone while I gaze at the ceiling wondering what I can wear that isn't black or partially black, my signature color.

Within seconds my screen explodes.

O.M.G.

Thousands of hits with "Salvador Torres" appear. Statistics, awards, images of Salvador kissing trophies that look taller than me. *Who is this man?*

My breath has more than left me. It's evaporated out of the atmosphere. I inhale deeply trying to find it again.

As soon as I can breathe properly, I choose an article about him and read it slowly. It tells me a lot about his football skills and nothing about him as a man. But that's what the images are for. I scroll through them and blink. Hard.

I can't count the number of different women on his arm in picture after picture. Some are celebrities. Major ones who star in vampire shows and win awards of their own.

Is he for real?

He's not the average player, that's for sure. On *or* off the field.

"Okay, Corrine," I pep talk myself. "Consider this your grand finale. After this date with Salvador Torres, you are done, girl. No more poor relationship choices.

"It's time to choose men of substance. Men with morals. Men who know the difference between a queen and a conquest."

"Right," I mutter. "I'm the queen. Not a darn conquest."

I sigh, remembering Salvador Torres in the flesh.

It's those Viking shoulders! I close my eyes and remember the handsome man towering over my five-foot-two frame. He was stuck in the middle seat of our three-hour flight from Porto and didn't complain.

The team's chartered plane had been canceled at the last minute and the players had to find seats wherever they could on our flight. He chose the one next to me after I'd smiled up at him innocently.

Yeah, right. More like a "come hither" look you gave to the ultimate alpha?

But the way he smelled. Spicy aftershave with a hint of baby powder. I sigh now recalling the details of the most epic meet cute of my life.

We talked (flirted?) nonstop in Portuguese so I could practice my language skills. Our conversation centered on football, food, and drinks.

His favorite drink, he said, is sangria and he told me about a bar in Porto, my new home city, called *Sangria Nights*.

"It's right on the water. You can see the bridge. And river

boats bring their cargo of wine from the Douro Valley vineyards straight to the bar. Sometimes, there are pirate-themed parties on the boats." His massive bone-crunching hands framed the scene for me as he grinned slyly. "I go as the best pirate of all."

"Johnny Depp?" I asked, innocently.

The look he gave me would sink a ship. "Um . . . no." He only said I'd have to see for myself.

It sounded fun. And a bit sketchy.

Kind of like Salvador Torres himself.

It didn't escape me that he never answered any personal questions. Like whether he was married? Or had a girlfriend? Or lived alone? Or live in Porto? Or what he did when he wasn't playing football and drinking sangria?

Avoiding personal questions is the sure sign of a bad boy.

Meanwhile, I shared all my details. Well, most of them. I didn't mention I'd scratched dating men like him off my life list for good.

When the plane landed, his large hands reached up and yanked down my bulging carry-on like it was a straw hat.

Then he formed a barrier with his body protecting me from other passengers reaching up to grab their bags above my head. As if he was ready to knock them out if they touched a single hair on my head.

Macho much? I wondered at the time.

Now I see. He's the supreme alpha male.

It doesn't matter though. Tonight, I'll enjoy myself at the game and the after-party. But that's it. I don't need to know anything personal about him. Because we're not going to see each other again.

What happens in Athens will have to stay in Athens.

AND BOY, MUST IT EVER. AS SOON AS I STEP OUT OF THE car and see that smiling, handsome face greeting me, I know I'm a goner. Can he get any more gorgeous in that sports jacket and perfectly sculpted jeans and . . . Italian shoes?

"You play football in those clothes?"

"Want to come with me to the locker room and find out?" he winks.

"Maybe. Are there others like you in there?" I put a hand on my hip and give him a brazen look.

"No," he growls. "No one's like me. And don't forget that."

Oh, shoot. Alpha is showing his teeth.

"That's cool. I came to see you play. No one else."

"Not even me?" shouts Danielo striding up and grabbing me in a hug. "Where's your sister?"

In one smooth move, Salvador extricates Danielo from my body and sets him back a few feet away. Salvador steps closer to me, bodyguard style. I'm not sure how I feel about all this "protectiveness."

Danielo grins and holds up his hands in surrender.

"*Desculpe*, my brother."

Salvador raises an eyebrow without smiling.

Danielo shrugs.

"She's gone over to Aegina. To make up with her boyfriend." I insert quickly into what appears to be a silent battle I know nothing about.

"My loss," Danielo says. "Enjoy the game, Corrine. It was nice to see you again." He swaggers off leaving me and Salvador standing closer than metro riders during rush hour.

"Isn't he your best friend?" I ask, tilting my face toward him.

"Yes, and?" Not a smile or wink in sight. Something has upset the man.

"Well, be nicer to him." We start walking toward a side entrance of the giant stadium. "It was just a hug."

"Right. Just a hug *today*."

I stop and turn toward him. "Are you . . . um . . . okay?"

I stop speaking when I notice the darkening in his grey eyes. Hurricane storm eyes. I was going to ask if he's for real. But I can tell he is. Somehow in the short time we've known each other, Salvador has appointed himself my savior/bodyguard. Whether I want one or not.

"I don't joke about who I'm dating. Not with my teammates." He says it calmly, but a hint of something dangerous lies in his undertone.

Dating? Is he talking about me? I'm just going to ignore that comment for now.

"Got it," I say. I tack a note onto my mental bulletin board — "*No joking with his teammates.*" Seems a bit extreme, but whatever. It's only for one night.

Salvador takes me to a seat in the VIP section where other spectators are walking around with wine glasses from a bar in the lounge area. It's very fancy and very cool and I feel a tiny bit out of my element. No one's my color; no one's my age; and no one's alone, which I will be very soon.

His phone is ringing like mad and I'm sure his coach or whoever is in charge must be wondering where their star player is.

"You need to go," I say, pushing his six-foot-four body (I read his stats) toward the elevator. It's like trying to move an elephant.

"Go," I whisper lightly. "I'll be okay. Thank you for this amazing opportunity to see a soccer—*football* match here." I indicate the luxurious lounge.

Salvador kisses my forehead before he hurries away to get ready. I barely noticed it. But a roomful of people did.

Since we arrived, they've been staring at us and whispering.

I examine the kiss as if it were a sip of vintage wine. Purposeful, with a hint of possessiveness and a gallant finish.

How did it make me feel?

Strangely, kind of normal. Like we're a couple. Which I know we are not.

"Are you the new '*It*' girl?" A blonde bombshell of a woman interrupts my kiss analysis. She has one arm crossed below her prominent chest propping up a glass of wine.

"Excuse me?"

"The '*It*' girl. The woman everyone wants. Especially Salvador Torres." She takes a big sip of wine and seems to be gurgling it around in her mouth. "You're not the first."

I feel the melanin drain right out of my face.

"Don't you speak English?"

I shake my head no. It's the only thing I can think of. Pretend I don't understand her.

She gives a rude *tut-tut* and marches away.

Wow! I look around for backup.

The bartender waves me over. He leans far forward and asks in English what I'd like to drink.

"Nothing," I say.

"You must have something. Mr. Torres asked me to take care of you."

I'm still mulling over that woman's words.

"Sangria," I say because it's the first thing that comes to mind.

The bartender's face lights up. "I should have known. It's Mr. Torres's favorite drink."

"How do you know that?" I ask.

He smiles as he pours red wine into a glass, along with some sparkling liquid and fruit.

"I travel with the team. I'm the older brother to one of the newest players. He's only seventeen, so my family sent me along to keep an eye on him. I like to mix drinks. Most arenas let me work the VIP bar. I'm a traveling bartender."

"That's cool. You get to travel, watch over your little brother, and meet new people. Plus, make money."

"Well, I only earn tips."

"Oh." I take a sip of the concoction he's created. My eyes open wide. "This is delicious. Not that I've tasted many sangrias before."

"It's the red wine that makes it taste so good. Finely aged Port from our city of Porto."

I hold the glass up to examine the red wine and the floating fruit toppers. "Yummy."

He laughs and extends a hand to me. "Miguel," he says.

"Corrine," I smile, shaking his hand.

After a few sips of my potent drink, I lean toward Miguel. I pitch my voice as low as I can and still be heard. "That woman over there," I point to the buxom blonde, "asked if I am the new 'It' girl. She said Salvador Torres has a thing for 'It' girls, which are women that many others want or something like that. What is she talking about?"

Miguel leans backward. He starts polishing glasses with a cloth. Glasses that look perfectly clean already.

"Did I say something wrong?"

He narrows his eyes at the woman. "Ignore her. I think she has a thing for Mr. Torres. Follows him around Europe to watch him play. Offers him gifts like cars and boats."

"People do that? They follow football players around like rock stars?"

A loud laugh erupts from my new friend Miguel. "Football players are bigger than rock stars in Europe. You'll see."

I put down my glass of sangria, which is surprisingly empty. "I'm not sure I want to see."

I search in my purse for some euro coins to tip Miguel.

He covers the tip bucket with his hand. "No. This is for Mr. Torres."

"I insist," I say, pushing his hand away. I drop five euros into the tip bucket. "I won't tell if you don't."

We share a laugh.

"I can see why he likes you."

I tilt my head. "Thanks."

I'm not sure being liked by Salvador Torres is a good thing though.

WATCHING MY FIRST-EVER FOOTBALL/SOCCER MATCH has me panting with exertion. My eyes and heart leap up and down the field with the Porto players, straining to catch every bit of fancy footwork and . . . well, let's face it, . . . a whole lot of veiny ripped leg muscles bulging under the hems of their uniform shorts.

I vow to cheer only for Porto in solidarity with it being my new hometown, but I fail miserably.

The Athens players resemble Greek gods commanding the field. It's very difficult to choose a side. Everyone deserves a cheer for scoring a goal, don't they?

Still, the one player who captures most of my attention is Salvador Torres. I see why the man is a legend. He roars onto the field and takes control every second he's there.

He never lets his guard down. He never fails to help up a fallen teammate. He's the first to congratulate a player who does anything well. He's the first to intervene between a player and the referee, or whatever those men running up and down the sidelines are called.

I get caught up in the crowd's excitement and find myself shouting and waving my arms in the air whenever one of Salvador's feet comes close to the ball. Along the way, I learn new Portuguese words that cannot be found in any language class.

I drink another of Miguel's delicious sangrias. To soothe my parched throat.

By the end of the game, I'm slightly tipsy. Salvador has scored two goals. And I've clapped my hands raw.

Most importantly, I can't look at Salvador again without contemplating his beefy thigh muscles.

Which sucks as I can't contemplate him at all after tonight.

A NEW SENSATION HITS ME WHEN SALVADOR EXITS THE locker rooms and beelines towards me, ignoring the press and paparazzi. Not butterflies in my stomach because I don't have shy nervousness. More like an elephant is stomping on my chest. The feeling is so strange I put my hand on my heart to protect it.

In moments, Salvador is standing before me grinning like a man who knows he's having a certain effect on a woman.

Cocky much?

"Well?" he asks.

That's when I see it. The little boy behind the alpha. He went all out tonight to impress me. To get my attention. It's there in the way his eyes hold a plea for praise.

I rise on my tippy toes to brush my lips on his stubbled cheek. "You were magnificent," I whisper.

I feel and hear flashbulbs popping all around us. Salvador continues to ignore them. I blink and lay my face against his soft jersey. He sweeps an arm around my waist to hold me against his tight hard body.

"That first goal was for you," he says firmly.

I grin up at him. "I and Porto thank you."

More flashes burst around us. "Who was the second goal for?" I'm joking, but a shadow crosses his features. He doesn't answer.

He presses me close instead, but I turn out of his embrace. Why does my heart feel as if someone stuck an ice pick in it?

Why is he behaving as if I'm the only woman in the room who he has eyes for, yet he won't reveal if he's single?

I could Google it, but I don't trust the sensational speculations that follow celebrities. And he's a celebrity over here.

Everywhere we walk, a camera snaps a photo. I'm glad my sisters and father don't follow European football news. In case tomorrow's sports headlines feature a photo of yours truly.

THE PARTY IS A FANCY AFFAIR. WOMEN ARRIVE DRESSED to the nines in short tight glittery dresses, stilettos, and designer handbags.

"You should've told me to dress up!" I smack my handsome escort on his arm as we stand on the steps of the entrance to an exclusive Athens club. The railings and doorway are covered with twinkly lights. Giant walls of men block the door checking off names on a list.

One of them sweeps his arm toward us to bypass the line and enter, but Salvador shakes his head. It seems he'd rather wait in line like everyone else—a move I mentally applaud.

"Anything but yellow and black.'" I mimic his earlier instructions.

He looks down confused. "You're the most beautiful woman here, Corrine. What are you talking about?'

I glance down at my striped blue and white pants, white one-shouldered top, and blue wrap that is draping across my arms. I'd researched Porto's team colors.

"I look like a sailor!"

He laughs loudly. People turn towards him, and I swear they want to bow as if he's King Carlos, former ruler of Portugal.

"Shh!" I nudge his midsection with an elbow. He doesn't flinch.

He glances at his watch. "Should we leave and go find you a gown, Cinderella?"

This time I'm the one laughing loudly. We get more curious glances and a lot of narrowed eyes throwing mental darts at me.

"I might need to use you as a human shield," I whisper loudly.

His arm wraps protectively around my shoulders. He looks down at me, grey eyes reflecting the twinkly lights around the club's entrance. "You have nothing to worry about. I'm not leaving your side."

"Well, let's hope I don't need to pee."

His deep chuckle raises goosebumps on my arms.

How can I walk away from this man?

But I must. "As soon as tonight is over," I warn myself. "Be prepared."

THE PARTY SURPRISES ME WITH ITS FOUNTAINS OF champagne, endless pitchers of sangria in honor of Porto's heritage, and a cake large enough for a person to leap out of, which I thought might happen, but thankfully doesn't.

"You are having fun, *querida*?"

"Did you call me 'sweetheart'?" I glance up at his face.

"You should know. You're the professional Portuguese translator," he grins.

"Not yet. I'm still working on it. I need clients!"

"You'll find plenty when you're living in Porto." He says it so confidently I can't help but believe him. It gives me a warm feeling knowing this supreme athlete, who must have worked very hard to get to his level of expertise, believes in me.

By the time we eat from a shared plate, clink glasses of sangria and say hello to teammates, coaches, and news reporters, it's time to leave. I'm literally drooping against his body.

The drive to my apartment is quick. Before I know it, he's helping me to my front door.

For the first time since we've met, Salvador looks unsure of himself. He's shifting from one foot to another but not in the professional way like he did on the field earlier.

"Thank you for an amazing evening," I say, smiling up at him.

When he doesn't make a move, I reach up and yank his jacket lapels, pulling his face close.

"I'm going to kiss you, okay?" I say looking into his eyes.

He nods wordlessly.

Inside I'm grinning.

I tiptoe. *This is the end of your era of bad boys, Corrine. Make it good.*

I close my eyes and kiss his wide firm lips like it's the last kiss I'll ever have.

My lips are hungry and searching. Before I know it, he grabs me up and lifts me right off my feet. My arms slip around his neck. I fall into his kiss as if it's a pool of deep water and I'll never swim out.

When he rests me gently back onto the ground, I eye this pirate kisser with a sad ache in my heart.

"Goodbye," I whisper.

He seems to catch the depth of my words and the meaning behind the kiss.

"I'll see you in Porto, right?" he asks, fear crowding his eyes.

I don't answer. I slip inside the apartment and close the door firmly behind me.

No one is more surprised than me at the tears I catch rolling down my face.

Chapter One

The city of Porto, tucked between the wild northern Atlantic Ocean and the emerald green vineyards of the Douro Valley, has awakened some dormant spirit inside of me.

Is this what travel can do to you? Stir up parts of you that you didn't realize were waiting to be awakened, like Sleeping Beauty waiting for her true love's kiss.

If that's the case, then Porto is my Prince Charming.

And Porto certainly feels like my personal prince. Putting aside that the man I am trying to avoid at all costs lives somewhere on one of these traditional streets and that I could bump into him at any second.

My favorite place to walk in Porto is *Rua das Flores* or Street of Flowers. I figure it's the last place a notoriously famous football star would venture. One, it has a lot of tourists. Two, it's so cute!

The pedestrian-friendly pathway is home to elegant five-story buildings with fine wrought-iron balconies overflowing with flowers. The buildings date from the 17th to the 19th centuries and were once homes of the Portuguese aristocracy.

Now they house cafés, bars, and my favorite *pastelaria*, where I stop for my morning coffee and *pastéis de nata*, Portugal's famous custard tarts. Every time I sink my teeth into the flaky crust I can't help but wonder if he likes them too.

I always wave that traitorous thought away and continue taking slow bites, chewing purposefully, ridding my mind of a tall handsome footballer with a wickedly sexy smile.

Chapter Two

On the last day of September, about one month after I settled into my apartment, started my classes at the University of Porto, and embraced my life as an international student, I longed to sit outdoors at my favorite *pasteleria*. It's the first crisp fall day after a very hot month.

But, the outdoor seating is full even though it's only 8 a.m. So, I cram my body and bag of books into a corner inside and stare out the window at the late-blooming flowers adorning the balconies. They speak to my soul.

In fact, almost everything about Porto makes me feel as if I'm living in a dreamscape. Bookshops and libraries sprout here as plentiful as the flowers.

I can be in a century-old bookstore in the morning, deep in its dungeon of classical Portuguese texts that need translating into English, then in the afternoon, climbing the famous staircase of the Livaria Lello, also known as the Harry Potter bookstore.

On especially sunny days, I can jump on a rented bicycle and pedal for twenty minutes to the sea, spreading a blanket on ancient rocks and cooling off in one of the many rock pools conveniently provided by the Atlantic Ocean.

My family home is on the opposite side of this ocean in

Maine. Somehow, it's completely different in Portugal. For one, the surf scene attracts internationally renowned surfers to ride the waves breaking offshore.

Did anyone say "surfers?"

Surfers = bad boys = not for me, Corrine Walker.

The same goes for soccer stars.

Fortunately, I have not run into my personal catnip in Porto.

During my first month of living the dream amongst Porto's stylish restaurants, museums, beaches, and bars, I managed to avoid being in the same place as Salvador Torres.

Now, crammed into my little corner, I slide the last bits of pastry into my mouth and close my eyes to savor the creamy goodness. I could eat one every single day. Actually, I *do* eat one every single day!

And why not? I'm getting loads of exercise walking the hilly streets that circle this city.

Porto is extremely walkable, from the riverbanks to the highest church-perched hill. A walk I just finished this morning before the sun blazed into the sky and sparked its beams onto the Duoro River.

I open my book after wiping my gooey fingers on a napkin. I have almost two hours before my first class and plenty of time to read and translate a chapter before I have to go.

It's only an eleven-minute walk to the University of Porto. I have timed it perfectly.

Chapter Three

I signal the server for another coffee.

I also survey every table to make sure Salvador is not here. It's become a habit now. Not a good one, I'd say.

Every time I slide my eyes over a group of people, whether outdoors listening to sidewalk musicians or inside my favorite cafe like now, my heart speeds up.

And I know it's not from the strong caffeine. It's because the part of me that doesn't want to see him is at war with the part of me that does.

Why else do I walk all over Porto every day?

Exercise? Sure.

To engage with the city's beauty. Of course.

To possibly run into Salvador Torres? Um . . . no . . . yes . . . maybe.

But I'm fighting it, aren't I?

It's not as if I'm a wimp willing to cave at the sight of smoldering eyes and a sexy stubbled chin. Viking shoulders. Broad chest. Muscled thighs with ridges of veins that ripple like the undulations of the Douro River.

I am officially breaking a bad habit. In my case, dating and falling into bad relationships is a habit that can and will be broken.

I will say NO. I will push away Prince Charming if he shows up, or rather, *when* he shows up, surrounded by legions of women fighting over him.

Porto is not that large. Salvador Torres *is* Porto.

I see his face and hear his voice everywhere I go. On television screens in bars when football games are being aired. On the Portuguese radio station that I turn on every morning to perfect my language skills.

He is *everywhere.*

I take one more glance around the *pastelaria* to make sure he isn't hovering nearby. Not that he could hover. The man is a walking European superstar, bigger than Drake back home.

How hard is it to turn a cold shoulder to a sexy giant of a man with twinkling eyes whose celebrated football skills are overshadowed only by his charm?

Easy peasy!

"Excuse me, miss?" The server's voice is hesitant.

I look up with an innocent expression to hide the creepy celebrity crush vibe I may be giving off.

My server is a young man with a sunburned complexion, deep dark blue eyes, and hair the color of wheat. He must be a foreign student like me.

He stares warily at the open textbook, notebook, and phone on the tiny table. There's no room for my coffee with all my gear.

I slide the notebook into my lap and accept the coffee.

"*Obrigado.*" I smile up at his handsome face. Now here is a nice guy for one of my baby sisters. Maybe Daisy. She'd love Porto's romantic essence.

Emerald would find it wasteful with its excessive beauty. She'd prefer something she could fix up and make better for humanity.

Maybe I always knew I belonged here. That's why I studied the Portuguese language for years to become fluent. Even when I didn't have to, because the boy I was learning it for ran off and left me.

For unknown reasons, my dream has been to live here and walk these old streets and eat these divine foods.

Not to mention the coffee! Strong Portuguese coffee is the only way to start the day.

I take a spine-stiffening sip and remind myself, "You're here to study. To practice your translating skills. To . . ." I stop. Salvador's gorgeous smile has popped up on the television screen behind the counter.

He waves a hand at an interviewer, then wraps a muscled arm around the poor guy's thin shoulders and bends his glorious head of spiky hair toward the mic.

I can't hear his thickly accented voice. I can't read his lips, stare as I do at their luscious curves. But I can read the Portuguese words that appear below him.

"I'm happy to be back in my hometown. I'm not leaving until we secure our victory."

A loud cheer goes up behind him as the camera angle tracks the fans, ten people deep spreading out around Salvador like his own personal sun rays.

The interviewer poses another question. Something about whether he's single or . . . available or . . . hmmm . . . a word I don't recognize.

Before I can look it up, I hear Salvador's deep voice clearly as the din of the cafe dies down and everyone stares at the home-town hero.

In English, he says, "I'll leave a ticket for you at the gate. Please come!" He stares magnetically right at me as if he can see me sitting here watching him.

I gasp.

A loud cheering rises up behind him. Followed by shrieks in many languages of, "I love you, Salvador!"

I catch a glimpse of his best friend Danielo being interviewed behind Salvador. These guys are never far apart.

When the show moves on to other news, I collapse into my tiny chair, not realizing I'd frozen in place during Salvador's guest appearance on screen. I bend my stiff neck from side to side.

"You okay?" my server asks, pointing to my empty cup.

I shake my head. "No. But I will be. Can I please have another *pastéis de nata?*"

When in doubt, pastry up.

I know all about eating my feelings as I did it a lot when I was twelve and no one, not one single member of my family, knew I was stuffing my face and throwing up late at night.

By the time anyone figured out to ask me if I was okay — my grades and school attendance never slipped — I was fourteen going on fifteen and replaced food with boys, the more unsuitable the better.

I like to think I chewed them up and spit them out too. Sadly, it was the other way around.

This is why Portugal is my chance to reinvent myself. To be the new and improved Corrine Walker. The woman focused on her own needs and goals.

I am proud I've managed to find better ways to deal with feelings of loss and despair. Now, eating is a joy and not a disease. But I stay vigilant.

This giant of an athlete with his crinkling eyes and beguiling smile will not steer me off course.

He can take his free football tickets and his suave, debonair charm and hightail it somewhere far away. Like up the Douro River with the river boats.

Chapter Four

Speaking of riverboats, I can see them clearly from the window of my cute apartment on Porto's riverfront.

They chug up and down, with barrels of port loaded on them looking very *Pirates of the Caribbean*.

With no other buildings blocking my view, I can see across the river to Vila Nova de Gaia, where the famous port houses and cellars have taken up residence on the hillside for centuries. Their name brand signs announce their heritage as much as their products.

But it's not the port houses or boats, or the shirtless, dockside guitarist that catches my attention when I lean out the opened windows.

Nope. It's the Dom Luís I bridge.

Spanning the river with its majestic arch, and its walkway for pedestrians who like their walks high and windy, I marvel at the architectural wonder.

This bridge represents something to me. I'm just not sure what it is yet.

Nothing as cliché as a bridge to my future.

Or a bridge to my past.

Or even a bridge to access the best, inexpensive port on the other side of the river.

Nope, this bridge with its golden arches, lit up at night like half of a halo fallen to earth, represents something more significant.

Something deep and personal and spiritual.

It could be that King Luis I was a Portuguese-English translator like me.

He translated *Hamlet* into Portuguese, no small feat. And the highlight of his reign was being the first person to bring fully translated Shakespeare plays to Portugal.

How cool is that?

When I can translate Shakespeare's plays into Portuguese, I'll let you know.

This connection to the Portuguese king may be why I said yes to this apartment as soon as I saw its proximity to the beautiful bridge built in his honor.

The only negative is that the tiny studio costs twice as much as I budgeted for housing when I mapped out my expenses for my year abroad.

This means I eat less, drink less, walk more, and try to save euros everywhere I go. In Porto, wine is cheaper than water, so there's that.

Sangria is the best as it's wine plus sparkling water, so it serves two purposes.

But my apartment, as enticingly close to the Dom Luís I as I can get, has left me in a clutch.

I need a job. My student visa allows me to work 20 hours per week.

This is how I find myself answering an ad for an English tutor paying an obscene amount of money. Like *obscene.*

I'm sure many will apply, and the job will be given to someone with actual tutoring experience.

Me, I tutored my sisters, but no one else.

I was too busy dating the bad boys and dealing with the

draining emotional fallout of pretending it was a passing phase and no need to mention it to the therapist who was helping me overcome my eating disorder.

One problem at a time, please.

Plus, I was *fine!* Seriously, was dating morally gray guys even treatable?

Not according to the *Vampire Diaries.*

I handled it then. I can handle it now. If avoiding the object of my reluctant affection, Salvador Torres, can be called "handling" anything.

Chapter Five

It's Saturday morning. The football game has come and gone, and I did not leave my apartment in case I was tempted to show up outside Porto's stadium flashing my identification and picking up a ticket I believe was sitting there in my name.

I could be wrong.

Salvador must have other English-speaking friends in Porto. I can't be that important or special to this international superstar.

I checked his social media pages when we first met. The man has more followers than the population of cities on the Eastern United States seaboard.

I'm a leaf, a flower, a ripple in his pool of admirers.

"Olá," I say into the phone after the number rings and rings and finally an answering service picks up.

"This is Corrine Walker. I am applying for the position of . . ."

The machine blurts, "This mailbox is full."

Great. It was too good to be true.

I tear my eyes away from Dom Luís I and back onto the help-wanted classifieds in Porto's online job search site.

I'm clicking on jobs like my life depends upon it, which it

does, when my phone WhatsApp beeps. A message from a strange Portuguese number appears.

"Interviews for the English tutor job at 2 p.m. at the park across from the Torre dos Clérigos."

I stare at the message, brows puckering. They want to meet across from the famous church tower landmark.

Okay, but where in the park? Is this legit? How will I know who to meet? Is this a scam?

As these thoughts race through my head, another message pops up. "Due to the sensitive nature of this tutoring job, please come alone. Be ready to sign a non-disclosure form."

WTH!

I shake my head at Dom Luis I. "Can I trust this?"

The bridge hums with activity but says nothing meaningful back to me.

A knock on my door interrupts my communing with the steel structure hanging over the river.

"Woo hoo, it's Sylvia."

I grin. "Coming."

I swing open the door for my neighbor, Sylvia. She checks up on me like clockwork. Thinks I'm too young to be alone in a strange city.

She may have a point based on this sketchy interview I'm heading out to.

But I can't ignore it. The few hours it demands plus its high pay would save my butt for the entire year.

Chapter Six

"Hi there, Sylvia, where are you going today?"

Sylvia is a vision. Sixty years old with piles of thick dark hair framing an oval face and enormous brown eyes sheltered by the longest natural eyelashes I've ever seen.

She's always dressed in the latest fashions. Handbags that cost more than my college tuition swinging from her slim arm. She was a designer's assistant for years she told me.

She smiles like a little girl caught playing dress-up. "It's a secret."

"Oh, a secret admirer?"

She shakes and then nods her head. "From the '*Age is Just a Number*' dating site."

I clap my hands in front of my mouth. "You did it!" I wave her inside and make her sit down next to the open window where a glorious breeze is stirring up my papers.

She props her bag on her lap and winks at me. "You helped. It's your fault. Plus, I already know him. He's a blast from my past. I'm not going out with a stranger."

Sylvia and I bonded over our single status the first week I

moved in. I was lugging my suitcase up the steep stairs when she asked where my boyfriend was.

She cautioned me to take my time dating after I explained my bad-boy dilemma. "But don't wait too long. Love is our natural state of being. Your heart yearns to be in love."

Spoken like the true poet she is. We also bonded over our shared love for books.

I, in turn, advised her that it's never too late to find love.

I found this great dating site that I wished we had in the States for people of all ages to disregard age and race and other so-called obstacles and plunge in with hearts open.

I loved the philosophy behind the dating site and helped Sylvia set up her profile.

"I can't believe it worked."

"We don't know if it worked. I have a date. That's all." Her grin says it's more than that.

"Wait a minute. Is this the man you knew long ago? When you were nineteen? And he was . . . twenty-five? The bass player in the band that left for Australia?"

A blush rises on her cheeks. "And he didn't come back. You remember all of that?"

I nod excitedly. "Of course, I remember. You're the only one of us in the dating pool right now. I have to live through you."

She chuckles and I smile. I feel a connection to Sylvia the way I do to Dom Luís I. Like I'm supposed to be here with them both.

"Do you need me to be your wing woman?"

She frowns.

"It's like a friend who tags along. Just in case."

She flashes her sparkling white teeth. "We're going to see a band performing in the park." She names a park by the beach miles away.

If I didn't love Sylvia I'd feel total envy. She's reconnected with a long-lost love. At the same time, I'm swearing off toxic relationships and hiding from a very strong temptation.

"You're going to have a great time," I tell her reaching over to give her a tiny hug. "I don't want to mess up your makeup."

I feel water pricking my eyelids. I'm not an overly sentimental sort, not like Ava or Daisy. But in one month of knowing Sylvia, I care about her as if she were my own mother.

I have never thought that way about anyone else in my life. Even now a twinge of guilt shoots through me like I'm cheating on Mom.

Sylvia must sense something weird happening inside me. She stands up and throws her arms around me. "Makeup is just face coloring. Heart coloring is more important." She wraps me closer and I sigh softly.

It feels strange to be hugged by a woman who could be my mother. If I'd been born here. It almost feels as if something missing from my life isn't missing so much anymore.

When she steps away she continues to hold my arms like she's checking me over for bruises.

It makes me realize how much I've missed out on not having a mother check on me and hug me even when dressed up and heading somewhere important.

At that moment, the sun hits Dom Luís I just so. The golden rays glint off the bridge's arch and shine into the window gathering me and Sylvia into a circle of light.

If I were the sentimental sort, I'd think Dom Luís I was channeling Mom's glow and energy, sending her waves of love onto me.

But I'm not Daisy with her poems and her sonnets. I'm me. Practical, forceful, and ready for this interview. It's a stepping stone to a successful year abroad. To a career as an international translator.

I'm going to get this job.

Just like Sylvia is going to get her first love back.

And that is that.

Chapter Seven

But that isn't quite that at all.

I arrive at the park across from the famous building. I crane my neck to see the top of the stone tower.

I plan to get up there one day.

I'm kind of afraid of heights. Okay, a lot afraid. So this tower hasn't been high on my list of places to visit.

The sky above the tower is a solid blue canvas, with birds in formation zipping toward the river.

The sun glints off their silvery wings. The sunshine hits hard here even though it's the beginning of October.

Back home in Maine, I'd be wearing sweaters and leggings. Probably a jacket too.

For my interview, I've put on a short-sleeved khaki dress with buttons down the front and pockets. Of course pockets! I won't wear a dress without them.

I'm a half hour early so I find a seat at the end of a long table near the busy bar in the park.

Metal watering cans with flowers tied to their handles are everywhere on the tables and the grass next to lounge chairs. They are "ice buckets" holding bottles of wine. Truly original.

I wish I could order my own watering can of wine. Any one of Portugal's delicious inexpensive wines would do.

Instead, I take out the book I'm translating by the Portuguese Nobel Prize-winning author José Saramago. It's on loan from the old bookshop I discovered on *Rua das Flores*.

I don't want to take out my notebook and try to write with all the wine sloshing about nearby so I settle down to read the book quietly.

Every few minutes I glance across the street at the sidewalk in front of the tower. In case the mysterious interviewer appears with a sign.

Like when you exit the airport and a driver is holding up your name on a card.

My backpack is open at my feet so I can quickly toss my novel in and zoom over there. I want to be first in line.

It's the only way to get this coveted job that pays a ridiculous amount of money.

I'm daydreaming about the beautifully painted tiles I'll buy with the money from my new job when I hear a loud voice shouting in my direction.

"Watch out!"

Chapter Eight

"**W**hat?" I shriek.

"No!" One of the waiters runs towards my table. "Catch him."

A horrible thought enters my head. I've seen way too many Jason Bourne movies.

I jump up. "Catch who?"

The waiter is still running toward me. But now he's pointing.

People are leaping up and squealing. This is not good.

I jump up on the bench as more people squeal. I get a look at the chaos around me.

A small furry animal is dashing around knocking over buckets of wine, tipping over wine glasses at a manic rate, and leaping over legs, bags, and bean bag chairs like it's auditioning for a circus role.

Is it a rat? A cat? Something indigenous to Portugal like a wombat is to Australia?

My ears pick up on the word "cachorro," which everyone is yelling.

As my brain is registering that it's just an innocent puppy racing around loose, the furry brown animal dives into my open backpack and disappears.

The waiter chasing it slides to a halt. Everyone is looking at me as if this disaster is all my fault.

"He's not mine!" I cry.

I jump down from the bench and move timidly toward the squirming backpack.

In utter horror, I watch as my backpack tips over. My beautifully printed resumes slide out covered in muddy paw prints.

No!" I stare at my future in dismay.

At the sound of my voice, the furry brown head pops up. A long pink tongue lolls out the side of its mouth. The puppy is panting faster than my heart is racing.

"Whose dog is this?" I ask, gazing left and right. "Can you please come and get it?"

The puppy eyes me and ducks back into the backpack as if hiding from everyone.

His tail pokes out swishing like he's happy he found a refuge.

I'm not going to touch the backpack. I don't know if he's had his shots. If he's going to bite me.

I don't know anything about dogs. Especially ones that perform like escape artists amongst dozens of lawn sitters.

I glance around at the folks heading to the bar to replenish their watering cans of bottled wine and their empty wine glasses.

"Can you help me?" I call out to the waiter.

He points to the busy bar counter. "Sorry," he says as he ducks back behind the bar. "Give me a few minutes."

No one else is paying any mind to me.

What the hell!

My backpack has quieted down. He better not be sleeping in there.

Chapter Nine

A young woman about my age, early twenties, stops on her way to the bar. She gives me a sympathetic look. "I think he's a stray. We tried to catch him last week, but he disappeared fast."

She points at my backpack. "Looks like he found where he wants to be."

"No way." My hand grips my heart. "I'm not a dog person."

At that moment loud snoring sounds emerge from my backpack.

The woman chuckles and leaves.

"Oh, my goodness. This isn't happening."

I pull my phone out of my handy dress pocket.

Ten minutes. I have ten minutes to fix this situation and get over to the tower for my interview.

Who can I call to help me out?

My phone swings helplessly from the wrist strap. No one! I have no one to call to get a dog out of my backpack so that I can go to my interview.

An image of Salvador in sexy black jeans and expensive sunglasses perched on his forehead blinks like a neon light in my mind.

No! Not him. Definitely not him.

I can't leave my backpack here. It's got my wallet, IDs, and keys inside.

I nibble on the edge of my thumb and glance across the narrow street.

Is that a line forming? I can't tell if it's an overflow of people to get into the tower. Or a line for the job interview.

Who interviews people on the street anyway? Nothing is making sense today.

I heave out a big sigh and frown down at my backpack.

"Look mister, you have to go sleep somewhere else."

Nothing. Not even a puppy snore.

"Are you okay?" a young man comes over and holds out a glass of wine for me to take. "It's from the bartender. He said you may need this."

I glance across the lawn. The bartender is smiling at me. He shrugs his shoulders and points at the bag at my feet.

If I wasn't so stressed, I'd smile back. He looks harmless enough. Like a student trying to earn some money on the side.

Kind of what I'm trying to do right now.

I accept the wine and take a sip of the cold refreshing drink. It's the liquid courage I need for what I have to do next.

I put the glass down on the table and scoop up my backpack carefully. I hurry over to a line of shoulder-height flowering bushes.

I stoop down, put my phone on the grass, grip the backpack securely with both hands and turn it over.

The puppy tumbles out in a heap of brown fur and pink paws smeared with dirt. He blinks at me.

We stare at each other for a few seconds. He looks so sweet and innocent. Nothing like the little monster who destroyed half a bar a few minutes ago.

"What?" I say to his furrowed forehead.

A low whimper.

"Sorry dude, I have places I need to be."

I reach over to rub his little head when, quick as a mood change, he leaps into the air like a jack in the box before dropping down on all fours.

Before I can stand up and get away, he springs onto my phone case.

"No!" I yell. "Bad boy."

It's too late. The strap is between his teeth. My phone dangles from his jaws.

He shakes his head back and forth like he's daring me to come and get it.

"Give it back. You bad, bad boy!"

Brown furry ears flicker as if he's considering it. Then in a flash, he disappears under the bushes, phone and all.

Chapter Ten

I dive onto the grass like I'm sliding into home base.

I push my way under the bushes following the pile of brown fur as far as I can go.

My shoulders are scratched from low-hanging branches. My head pounds from the loud puppy barks this monster is making in my ears.

"Come here!" I reach out a hand and try to grab his leg. When I catch hold and pull he yelps so pitifully I release him.

I forget where I am and try to sit up only to bang my head on a really hard branch.

Hot tears tip out of my eyes and roll down my cheeks.

"I need my phone," I cry at the ball of fur just out of my reach.

My dress is scrunched up to my hips. My bare legs are sticking out from the bushes. I can imagine the sight of me right now. But I don't care. I can't leave.

"You are awful, you know that?"

"Arf! Arf!" the puppy's barks are joyous. Typical bad boy with no clue how much madness he's causing.

"You are so bad."

"Arf! Arf!" he agrees.

He lays down on top of my phone and starts digging hard.

Dirt flies into my face. Into my mouth and nose and eyes.

I swear under my breath and hurl myself forward, eyes closed, patting the ground wildly and blindly with one hand.

"I'm going to drag your backside out of here one way or another."

"Excuse me, miss, can I help you?"

What the hell!

My eyes are closed so dirt doesn't get into them and I can't tell if the voice is coming from behind me or next to me. I'm all kind of confused right now.

"Yes," I choke out. "I need help. This dog has my phone."

A chuckle that is vaguely familiar sounds in my ear.

"Okay, you slide back out and I'll reach for him, okay?"

"Okay," I say with relief. I think it must be the bartender. He must have seen me crawl under the bushes and come to help.

But why does this voice sound so deep and mature and . . . familiar?

I slide out and sit up. I chase dirt from my cheeks. Dust particles from my eyelashes.

When I open my eyes, a small child is staring at me from mere inches away.

I lean back. "Arrrrgh! Who are you? You scared me."

The little girl of about six or seven, stands with her hands on her hips and a skeptical look stitching her eyebrows together.

"You're the one who's scaring everybody."

Her matter-of-fact tone forces me to agree. "Yes, you're right. I'm sorry. I didn't mean to scream."

At that moment, the legs and broad back of a giant of a man emerge from under the bushes.

In one large hand, he's dangling the bling strap of my beloved phone.

In his other hand, he's grasping the ruff of the little dog.

"Why's he crying, Daddy? What did you do to him?" The

puppy is indeed whimpering as if his little heart is broken in two. Which it might be when I'm done chastising him.

But neither the phone nor the puppy is what makes my jaw drop open until it's almost hitting my chest.

Because standing before me, tall, handsome, and muscled, holding the puppy like it's a baby now, is none other than Salvador Torres, Porto FC's superstar player.

And gripping the fingers of one of his large hands is the girl, who's still calling him, "Daddy."

I drop back onto my heels.

This time it's me who's whimpering.

My poor heart can't take any more surprises.

Chapter Eleven

Some people love surprises. I am not one of them.

Some people say they don't like surprises but secretly hope their friends, family, and boyfriend will throw them a big party or give them an unexpected gift.

Not me.

I like to manage my life carefully. I schedule my homework and my progress every day.

I have an outline for each day and I know where I'll be, when, and how I'll get there.

My sisters tease me that I can't survive without my color-coded planner.

They're right.

It started when I was eleven years old while Mom was sick. My eldest sister Ava was busy researching cures for cancer and trying to get Mom and Dad on board with different holistic practices.

I began keeping track of Mom's doctor visits. Her chemo schedules. I kept colorful sticky notes for progress and highlights. Eventually, the sticky notes dwindled to nothing.

Mom passed away on a horrible cold gray morning. No amount of planning could stop it.

Every day after that, I woke up to a gaping hole of nothingness.

In various rooms and corners of our house, I could hear one or more of my four sisters crying.

I could hear one of my aunts talking softly on their phones whispering about the plight of this poor man (my father) and his five motherless daughters.

Ava was only fourteen, but after my aunts departed one by one, she took over organizing our lives. The house, the food shopping, the laundry, all while still attending school.

Ava was so busy she had no time for any kind of life outside of the family. That's why she didn't have a boyfriend until she was twenty-five!

Bridget my next oldest sister was Ms. Popular starring in every play and musical in middle then high school. Bridget thrived on being unavailable to any guy who liked her for more than a hot minute. That finally changed months ago when she went to visit an olive farmer on a Greek island.

Our baby sisters, Daisy and Emerald, needed the most attention from our father and Ava. Daisy was seven and Emerald was six when Mom died.

As for me, the middle sister, I could see what was going on from both sides. My older sisters were busy and stressed out. My baby sisters were frightened and sad.

I learned to keep my head down and not cause any problems for anyone.

This is how my trusty notebooks evolved into detailed calendars for my life. My planning didn't save Mom, but it saves me from stress of the unpredictable.

Some folks have security blankets, I have notebooks.

They give me a much-needed peace of mind and a grounded feeling of being in control.

Which is why I Do Not Like surprises.

Chapter Twelve

Salvador Torres with his late afternoon stubble, sparkly gray eyes, cute daughter, and scruffy puppy held aloft is definitely a surprise and *not* a part of my plans.

I look wildly around to the other side of the street where my job interview should be taking place right now.

My watch says it's after 2 p.m. Ten minutes after so I'm late. But there's no sign of anyone interviewing people. I squint my eyes against the sunshine as I scan the sidewalk.

"Where are they?" I mumble to myself. "Surely they can't have finished already."

"Who are you talking to?" His voice is like I remember it from my dreams. Deep and confident.

I swallow and stand up slowly, dusting off the grass and dirt from my dress.

"I'm sorry. Thanks for getting my phone back." I reach for the object spinning from one of his fingers.

He grunts and rests it in my hand.

"Who's this, Daddy?" The girl is speaking in Portuguese. I get a good look at the little minx and she's the spitting image of her father.

Both have blondish brown spiky hair, although hers is pulled back in a ponytail but there are stray strands sticking out all over.

Both have the same greyish-brown eyes. Is that even a color?

And both have the same tilted head, quizzical look right now as they take in my disheveled appearance. She's his mini-me for sure.

"Hi, I'm Corrine." I extend my hand to shake hers. She quickly grips mine in hers and gives me a gap-toothed smile.

"I'm Isabel. But you can call me Izzy."

"Nice to meet you, Izzy."

"And this is Daddy." She raises up his hand that she's holding to extend it towards me to shake. Like he's her puppet.

I never thought I'd ever see the famous Salvador Torres being bossed around by a woman, much less a tiny little thing like Izzy.

I smile and take his proffered hand.

"Nice to meet you again, *Daddy*."

I'm dying to ask him why he didn't tell me he had a daughter. We spent an entire plane ride seated next to each other plus a night on the town in Athens on a date. This is important information.

I scowl at myself while thinking about that. I don't like to share my personal information, especially my mental health struggles with just anyone. Maybe he feels the same way about being a parent.

He grins and I forget about any potential red flags. (Hint to self, ignoring red flags is how you end up dating bad boys.)

He squeezes my fingers. "Enchanted. Here's your *puppy*." He shoves the little monster into my arms.

I immediately drop it to the ground. "He's not mine. He's a stray dog. He could have a disease or something."

Salvador frowns at the pup who's sitting with chubby legs askew. The dog's head is tilted to one side, and a lone ear pokes up like he's indignant that I'd accuse him of being diseased.

"You hurt his feelings," Izzy cries, bending down to pat his head.

I would roll my eyes if I didn't think the exact same thing.

"You may be right. I'm sorry. I didn't mean it." I lean over and join her in patting his small head. The puppy flops onto the grass and shows us his pink belly.

Izzy and I grin at each other. She rubs his little tummy. I flick his ears back and forth like I'm turning a light switch on and off.

He seems to love it. I swear he's purring like a cat.

"I like him, Daddy."

"I do, too." I smile at Izzy. She reminds me of my little sister Daisy, who adores her cat Freckles.

Izzy and I look up when Salvador steps forward, blocking out the sun. A frown the size of the Grand Canyon creases his handsome face.

"We can't have a pet right now, Iz, sorry. You know it's on our future bucket list."

"I hate our buckle list," she pouts standing up and wiping what I believe are fake tears from her eyes.

I've seen plenty of fake tears from my little sisters.

"It's a *bucket* list, honey, not buckle."

She sniffs.

Salvador reaches down with strong arms and scoops her up. To me, whispers, "Don't encourage her. I'm not really a pet person."

Again, I'd roll my eyes if I didn't feel the exact same way.

At that moment a loud squeal goes up by the bar. The three of us and the puppy swing around in surprise.

Heading our way are a group of about twenty or more people. They're waving flags, shirts, and scarves, and shouting Salvador's name.

Panic flashes in his eyes. He looks like he wants to pick me up in his other arm and run.

"Hurry," he hisses. "Follow me."

For no other reason than that I can't imagine leaving the puppy on the grass to be trampled by a swarm of football fans, I swipe up the dog like he's an American football and toss him into my open backpack.

I start running while still zipping it up and sliding it onto my shoulders.

"I'm coming." I race after one of the fastest athletes in Europe.

Right Corrine. You got this.

Chapter Thirteen

The puppy is scratching the dirt around my beautifully polished sandals. The ones with lace-up straps that match my khaki dress perfectly.

I pick up my feet fast before he ruins them.

"Stop! You're a bad boy." I scold the dog.

"He's not a bad dog," Izzy cries, climbing down from her father's arms and cuddling the puppy.

We're in the garden in front of my apartment. It was closer than Salvador's parked car.

He'd waited for me to catch up and I made an executive decision to run in this direction.

He followed, trusting me completely which says a lot for his character. But not much for mine.

Because there I was leading the wolf straight to my den.

With our head start and my knowing a few shortcuts, we managed to arrive in record time. I ushered Salvador and Izzy into the garden and shut the gate behind us, locking it in the process.

"Wow! I'm impressed." Salvador was barely panting while my breath was coming in short gasps as if I'd raced across Europe. "Look at you, acting like you've dodged mob scenes all your life."

I was huffing and puffing too hard to answer.

I plonked down onto a stone seat at the far end of the garden far away from where any passers-by could see us.

My backpack was squirming.

I zipped it open and out tumbled the puppy looking harassed. He shook his body from head to tail then surprisingly, leaped up and licked my face.

"Ugh!" I wiped away the wet trail he left behind. "Get down," I said in a fake stern voice. I hoped he'd take it as a warning.

That's when he started to dig in the dirt.

Salvador is looking around the garden, his arms free now that Izzy is playing tug of war with the dog.

"Is this your normal life?" I ask.

He runs a large hand through his hair, pushing it backward. I can smell oranges and musk and something else. Oh, yeah, baby powder. Now it makes sense.

"It's not always like this. I love my fans, I really do. But having a private life is difficult with people wanting autographs and selfies all the time."

"I can't imagine that at all. Must be hard."

He glances over at me, a sexy grin lighting up his eyes. I wish I could say it had no effect on me. I'd be lying. My entire body trembles in excitement like a pre-teen at a Taylor Swift concert. Good thing I'm seated.

"I wouldn't be where I am today without them buying tickets to see me play so I don't mind. Just not all the time like when I'm with my daughter or with my . . . *a* woman."

He gives me a look under lowered lashes like you know what I mean, right?

I ignore the look. There's too much going on right now to concentrate on what he might mean.

"Where are Izzy and the puppy?" I glance around in alarm.

Salvador points. "Right behind you."

I swivel around and tuck my feet away because the puppy is once again digging a hole, looking intent on destroying my sandals.

I throw a twig for him to fetch. He eyes me and the stick with disdain.

Right.

I turn back to Salvador.

"How do you hang out in Porto if you're always being mobbed by fans?"

"Why do you want to know?" he smiles. "You want to go out with me?"

I scoff, "I'm asking for a friend."

"Good answer. I have my favorite places. Restaurants and clubs where people don't approach me. My restaurant *Sangria Nights* is not far from here."

"Your personal hide out," I tease.

He grins. "It is. My best friend and I are co-owners. You'd like it. It's not a tourist trap. We aim for an authentic vibe."

"Maybe I'll check it out. One day."

"Well, let me know. I can get you a free drink."

"You had to buy your own bar in order to go out and not be mobbed?"

"Something like that. It was our dream growing up. As soon as I got my first big check, we bought it."

I nod. I can appreciate a man with a plan.

"We go to the beach a lot, too." Izzy pipes up from somewhere near my feet.

I bend down to see the puppy and the girl tugging on either end of the stick. He pretends to growl. She laughs her head off.

I smile up at Salvador. There's something about a child's laugh and puppy noises that would make anyone smile.

"What are we going to do about this dog?" I ask hesitantly. "He can't stay here."

The puppy drops the stick in his mouth and yelps at me.

"What? You can't!" I say to the furry face. His tongue hangs out and he stares at me with big eyes.

"You're hurting his feelings again," Izzy cries out. "Stop that."

"Yeah," Salvador echoes. "You're hurting his feelings. Some people just want a little attention."

"People?" I ask. "Or . . . puppies?"

He grins. "Both?"

"I'm sorry, guys. I've already messed up a lot today. I can't add hiding out a puppy to my list." I heave a sigh.

"What's wrong?" The immediate concern in Salvador's voice is palpable. His eyes darken to a smoky grey. "Did someone do something to you? Are you okay? Did you get hurt running over here? Is it my fault?"

Whoa. I hadn't expected him to be so . . . *caring*.

Salvador and I lock eyes.

"It'll sound silly."

He shakes his head back and forth. "Nothing you say would sound silly."

He lowers his voice. "Do you know how much I've searched this city for you? I never realized Porto was so large until I tried to find the one person I . . . ."

"You what?"

The grey smoke lifts from his eyes and I see something unexpected. "The one person I missed. You."

"What? You barely know me."

"I know a lot. Did you forget our three-hour conversation on the flight from Portugal to Greece?"

I remember us talking nonstop jumping topics like a hopscotch mat. But I can't recall any specific things.

The dialogue had flowed between us naturally. Even as passengers around us snoozed, Salvador and I never stopped talking about our lives.

Izzy is cooing and rolling on the grass with the puppy now. I'm concerned for her clothes, her skin, and her possible need for a tetanus shot.

"Shouldn't we try to separate these two?" I glance down at the girl and the dog.

He shakes his head. "You've been avoiding me here in Porto. Tell me why. I thought we had a connection in Athens."

"No, I wasn't avoiding you."

"Liar liar, pants on fire."

"What did you say?"

"You heard me," he whispers again. "Liar liar, pants on fire."

I have no idea what to say so I burst out laughing. "You're crazy."

"I'm Portuguese."

"That, too." He's so . . . extra and easy on the eyes, and he makes me feel . . . lighter. Safer.

But that can't be right. He's dangerous. Well, at least I thought he was until he showed up with a daughter and rescued a puppy. Not to mention gallantly snatched my phone from the jaws of death.

"Tell me why you messed up today," he asks gently.

I bite my lower lip and consider telling him the truth. Other than my wonderful neighbor, Sylvia, I don't have any close friends in Porto yet. And I can't tell Sylvia about money troubles. I don't want her to worry about me.

But him. He's not my neighbor. It's not like I'll be seeing him again. Or regularly anyway.

"Okay, I'll tell you, but you have to promise to help me do something about this puppy afterward."

He nods and I see promises in his eyes. But they don't look like they have anything to do with dogs.

Chapter Fourteen

As I start to share my worries with Salvador, a feeling of relief overtakes me. Like I've been wanting to talk to him for a long time.

The calm focused expression on his face encourages me to go deep. Deeper than I thought I'd go with a guy I don't know all that well.

But something about his easygoing manner, his charm, and his large cool hand that he places on my shoulder in solidarity makes me spill it all out.

"I rented this apartment in this prime location so I could see the river and the gorgeous Dom Luís I bridge."

"It *is* a beautiful spot," he nods.

"But I can barely afford it. It was irresponsible."

"Can't you move somewhere else?"

"No! I feel as if I belong here. Plus, I signed a nine-month lease."

"Oh," he frowns. "What can I do to help?"

I give him a side-eye. "I'm not asking for help. I'm just telling you why events today are not going my way. It's a mess!"

"Okay, which part of this story is the messy part?" he squeezes my shoulder.

I glance up and roll my eyes in a big way. He can't miss it.

"I was supposed to interview for a job I need. Like really need," I confess with some embarrassment. "That's why I was at the park today."

To bring some levity to the situation I playfully add, "On top of that, my favorite dress and shoes are ruined." I point to my clothing.

"All because of . . . him." I poke a toe at the squirming puppy who's now barking and prancing around with Izzy without a care in the world.

"So, you see? Today was a waste."

"It isn't."

"I feel it is."

He points to Izzy and the puppy playing in the garden. "I haven't heard her laugh this much in a long time."

"Oh." I smile at the little girl spinning in circles on the grass. "Not a waste then."

I wait a bit to see if he'll explain why she hasn't laughed in a while. And maybe explain where Izzy's mother is.

I already know he's single. He announced that a few times when I met him. He doesn't look like he'd lie about something like that. But then, I had no idea he had a child.

After a few beats, I ramble on, "Well, it's nice to see you again, and meet your . . . daughter? But I needed that job. I need to make some money . . . or else . . . I'll have to cut my year abroad short and only stay one semester."

"And break your lease?" he asks in a mock shocked voice. "Absolutely not!"

"Do you have any bright ideas?"

His eyebrows dip together fiercely. "Wait. Are you talking about that job where interviews were being held across the street by the tower?"

"*Yessss?* How do you know about that?"

"Because I'm the one who placed that ad."

"What?"

"I'm seeking an English tutor. My PA was weeding out applicants at the tower and taking the ones with promise to the cafe next to the tower to interview them."

"Are you . . . were you . . .." My eyes narrow. Did this egotistical maniac put out an ad so he could find me?

He catches on to what's going through my head. His eyes turn narrow and flinty. "You aren't thinking that I . . .."

I nod my head up and down.

He shakes his head from side to side. "I didn't know you needed a job. And I had no idea you would answer *my* job ad."

"Oh, so this . . .." I spin one arm in the air, making a big Ferris wheel circle encompassing him, me, Izzy, and the bad puppy. "Is a coincidence? You being there with your child, your dog, and your job offer? Is this a setup?"

"Whoa! That is *not* my dog."

The puppy whimpers loudly.

"Hush!" we both snap at the poor thing on the ground looking at us with big puppy dog eyes.

"Don't yell at him," Izzy snaps at us.

"Sorry," we mutter simultaneously.

"Well?" I ask.

"Ha! If I thought I'd find you by posting an ad for a tutor, I'd have done it when I got back to the city a month ago." His voice is a deep growly sound daring me to argue.

When I don't say anything, he softens his tone. "It was frustrating going to all the places I thought you'd be. Do you have any idea how many *libraries* there are in this city?"

A snort escapes me.

"What?" he raises one perfect eyebrow.

"You say *libraries* like it's a bad word."

He grunts. "Can I sit down?"

I indicate the space next to me on the stone bench. "Feel free."

"I thought you'd want to see me again. Was I the only one who felt something in our kiss?"

"I'm not going to lie to you," I whisper. "Our kiss was sizzling."

He grins. "Like fireworks."

I push at his strong arm. He barely moves.

"But . . .."

He puts a finger on my lips gently. "Please don't '*but*' our kiss."

The intensity in his eyes is exactly what I've seen in the eyes of those bad-boy anti-heroes on television.

My heart dips crazily down to my stomach. I bite my lip to stay focused on the situation.

I scoot back on the bench. "I won't deny our kiss was intense. But it's got to stay where it happened. In Athens. I'm here now in Portugal to study and work hard. I want to . . .."

"Be an international translator, I remember. Why do you think I searched for you in all those hoity-toity intellectual hubs all over Porto? I have to say, no one knew me there."

I burst out laughing. "Poor baby, you sound disappointed."

"It was humbling," he mutters. "Can't folks read fancy books *and* watch football?"

"Can't folks play football *and* read fancy books you mean? Apparently not."

We share a laugh. Izzy and the puppy stop playing to look at us. A moment later they're back to throwing and chasing sticks.

"You'll have a hard time separating those two, you know."

"What about us two?"

"I'm on a hiatus."

"A what? I've never heard of that word."

"You're ridiculous."

"No, please, educate me."

I raise my eyebrows and give him a meaningful look. "It'll cost you."

He rubs his hands together. "I sure hope so."

The look of glee on his handsome face has me backpedaling a tiny bit. "Are you really single?" I blurt out.

"Are you really single?" he counters.

"*Psssssh*! You first."

"Yes, I'm unattached," he lowers his voice. "It's no secret, just watch the news."

I'm dying to ask where Izzy's Mom is, but I don't want to pry.

"And you? Is there a *smart* man waiting for you back home?" He frowns. "Or here?"

"I wish."

He frowns.

"What I meant to say, is no, I'm not seeing someone else."

He leans closer. His entire body seems to wrap itself around mine even though he isn't touching me at all.

"So, we can date!" His words caress my ear.

I shake my head. "No. I'm going to be very busy."

"What about hanging out with Izzy and the puppy."

I lean backward. "Whose puppy?"

We both glance down at the miniature beast chewing on the hem of Salvador's pants.

"What the . . .." Salvador gently shakes his leg to dislodge the pup, who sits back on his haunches, staring at one then the other of us.

Meanwhile, Izzy climbs into her father's lap and yawns loudly.

"Can we keep him please?" she begs.

He snuggles her close. "We'll see," he murmurs as Izzy nods off safe and sound.

On the ground by my feet, the puppy is fast asleep too, snoring his doggie snores into the cool evening air.

"It looks like we're the only ones awake," I say, smiling at the scene even though I'm also worried about what comes next.

Chapter Fifteen

My obsession with needing to know what comes next started days after we buried Mom on a rainy morning that spring. Every day it rained. It was the rainiest spring on record for Portland, Maine.

In addition to homework, chores, and extracurricular activities, there was one other thing I kept track of in my notebooks that no one knew about. One other thing I could do so that there were no open slots in my schedule.

I kept track of boys.

That may seem kind of creepy and stalkerish. It wasn't. I kept track of television heartthrobs. I became obsessed with *Vampire Diaries* and fell in love with the baddest of the bad boys.

Forget Damon Salvatore. I longed for an Original baddie.

I studied the show as if I would be tested on it.

When the world around me was falling apart, I gripped my notebook in one hand, my pen in the other.

I detailed how the bad boys (in this case vampires) walked, talked, and shrugged nonchalantly after ripping out a throat or a heart.

Like nothing mattered. Easy peasy.

I secretly longed to be like them.

To not care about anything.

In reality, I cared about every single thing.

I obsessed over my grades so I wouldn't think about how this tragedy could happen to us.

Because why? Why did this happen to five girls who needed a mother so badly?

Eventually, the clenched fist holding my heart began to squeeze too tightly. I had trouble breathing. The only thing that made that feeling go away was eating as much as I could. Then forcing it all back up.

Eat, vomit, eat vomit, and repeat. The eating felt so wonderful. So freeing. As if I was a real baddie.

The vomiting was my self-inflicted punishment for being so bad.

I kept track of my eating and vomiting as if it were a daily scheduled event. Along with my bad boys on the screen. These two things gave me solace in the darkest of times.

I'm not shocked that no one in my family noticed. Everyone was coping the best they could.

Which is what I need to do now. I can't let myself fall for a guy who gives off the same bad-boy signals as the others I've dated in the past. Super confident, charming, and a master of his universe.

Although now, with his adorable baby girl on his lap, and having just saved a puppy, Salvador Torres is defying my assumptions more than just a little bit.

Chapter Sixteen

A rosy glow lights up the sky as the sun sets behind the bridge. The garden gives off real fairytale vibes as late-blooming flowers emit their perfumed scents and birds caw across the sky heading south.

Neither I, nor Salvador, want to break the spell.

I don't know about him, but I haven't felt so peaceful in a long time. Despite all that went wrong today, he's right, there's more that was good.

Okay, I didn't get the job.

I didn't follow my plans for today.

The past three hours were surprising as hell.

I don't like surprises.

But I'm not mad at myself. Or at this hunk sitting beside me.

I feel grateful. And happy. And hopeful.

Salvador stares at his phone intently. Scrolling and reading, his lips moving slightly, which is cute.

I don't feel like checking my phone. It'll only remind me of how much I'm not on schedule.

"Well, this is crazy," he prefaces, sliding his phone into his pocket.

"Hmmm?"

"My PA texted me."

I sit up straighter. "The same PA interviewing folks for your mysterious job?"

"It's not what you think," he says. "It's legitimate."

"Well, I almost interviewed. I can show you the text telling me where to show up. I even had beautifully printed resumes until this guy muddied them up." I nod at the sleeping heap of fur at my feet.

Salvador swings one of his long legs across the bench and turns toward me, carefully cradling Izzy. "He didn't hire anyone. He said no one fit our needs."

"Sorry to hear that."

What *are* his needs?

"I'll interview you now."

I stare at him. "You?" I sputter. "I can't work for you."

He stares back. "Why not? You said you needed a job. You said we can't date. So, it's not as if you have to worry about dating your boss."

The smirk on his face makes me want to smack him. Or laugh. Not sure which I want to do more.

I glare at him. "I don't need a job that badly."

"Then you'll be saying *adeus* to Dom Luís I over there." He eyes me in a game of bluff the bluffer.

"You're not as cute as you think," I say, a little meanly.

"That's fine. Maybe you're not as smart as *you* think."

I cross my arms over my chest and gaze out at the gorgeous span of iron designed by a student of Gustave Eiffel, the master-mind behind the Eiffel Tower in Paris. I don't want to move!

"Fine. I'm ready. Interview me!"

"I think you should stop being so hostile toward your future boss."

"Poke the bear and you'll find out."

He frowns. "I don't know what that means."

"I see why you need a tutor." I smother a giggle. It's not cool to make fun of his lack of knowledge of American idioms, I scold myself.

"I'm sorry." I rid my face of any smirks or telltale signs of hostility. "I do need this job. I don't know why I'm being so antagonistic towards you."

"Maybe because you *like* me?" He winks.

I shove him gently, so I don't wake up Izzy. "You're lucky your hands are full."

He snorts. "You mean *you're* lucky my hands are full."

I narrow my eyes. "Meaning?"

"Okay, Ms. Walker, please tell me a bit about your experience tutoring English to foreign students."

I watch him out of the corner of my eye.

Strikingly tall, athletic shoulders straining at his jersey, his large hands so tender and caring with Izzy in them. The man is nearly perfect to look at.

I swallow hard. "I started tutoring when I was fifteen years old in high school. He was an African student from Angola. He spoke only Portuguese. By the end of the school year, he could speak fluent English and I could speak almost fluent Portuguese."

A painful memory flits through my mind. I shut my eyes.

"Ahem," Salvador clears his throat. "I believe there's more to that story. But I'm only interested in the educational part."

"The educational part was great. It was a success. Next question."

"Yes, how do you feel about tutoring a six-year-old?"

I glance down at the heap of flyaway hair and cotton on his lap. "It's for Izzy?" My heart melts a tiny bit.

He nods slowly. "We need to learn English. I mean she needs to learn English."

"Why?" I ask, sensing a note of desperation in his voice that matches a buried pain in his eyes.

He shrugs. "That's not important. Are you interested in the job? It pays a lot."

"I saw what it pays. Are you serious?"

"Yes, of course. I don't falsely advertise."

I look him over. You sure don't, I think.

"So, it's a deal?"

"How many hours per week?" I ask.

He stares into my eyes. I don't know what he's searching for, but it feels as if he's digging into my soul.

"Let's start with six hours per week and see how that goes."

"Great." With the hourly rate he's paying, I won't need another job.

"Perfect." He reaches out a hand to shake. I grip it in one of mine.

His touch makes me jump. Electricity zips through me. He must feel it too because he's staring at our hands where we seem locked together.

I recall holding his large, callused hand in Athens, walking into that party, and feeling a thrill of excitement.

It feels the exact same way now.

"I guess we don't need all that glitz and glamor," he mumbles.

I hear him clearly. And he may be right.

Chapter Seventeen

Whenever my sisters refer to me as the "smart" one, I remember those years of hiding and eating. Thinking I could fill that big empty nothingness inside me left behind by Mom's death. Ha!

In high school, a counselor who was familiar with Ava and Bridget and knew our home situation took a deep interest in me. I thought it was because of my excellent grades.

It was not. She picked up on something no one else did. She was not afraid to stick her nose in my business.

She arranged for me to see a therapist — with Dad's authorization of course — but I never told any of my sisters why I was seeing a therapist.

They all assumed it was grief counseling. Which it was in its own way.

I learned that we all process grief differently. Apparently, my way was to figure out how to do as much damage to myself as possible without anyone knowing.

Through all of this, my passion for bad boys on the screen continued.

Once I started high school, I discovered real-life bad boys who mirrored, what I believed to be authentic bad boys as portrayed in the media.

The boys who didn't care. Bad boys like John Bender from *The Breakfast Club*. Jordan Catalano from *My So-Called Life*. Shows I watched with Mom in her final stages of cancer.

It's no surprise that upon recovering from my eating disorder, I switched gears and found a new way to self-harm.

Enough of the vampire baddies. I wanted a real boy to fall head over heels for.

One with a cool, devil-may-care grin. Smoldering eyes, flaring nostrils, and a tick in his cheek to show he was holding back some untapped intensity.

I wanted the shrug of indifference, the glare of disdain, the smirk of conceit.

Like any nerd worth her book money, I read up on how to find and date the cool rebel.

My fifteen-year-old self was determined to be a brand-new person, worthy of such a love. But what kind of new person could I be?

Not the innocent waif.

Not the damsel in distress.

Not the badass with an attitude.

I didn't want to go emo, goth, raver, jock, poser or elitist.

I had to choose my new personality carefully.

Now, as I look back, I realize that people evolve organically into who they're supposed to be.

But I didn't have time to evolve organically. I wanted immediate transformation.

The summer before my sophomore year of high school was my summer of change. I did an entire 180-degree turn of personality.

All I really wanted was to be someone other than the girl who'd lost her beloved mother and fallen apart inside.

Chapter Eighteen

When I walked through the doors of South Portland High School in the fall of my sophomore year, I'd accomplished my goal.

Wearing dark clothing, black high tops, glitter eyeshadow, and a big smile that showed I cared for everyone, I was the "cool girl" full of personality and vibes.

I'd read a famous book over the summer by Dale Carnegie called *How to Win Friends and Influence People*. It was an eye-opener.

The biggest takeaway for me was to remember people's names. That simple.

According to Mr. Carnegie, the favorite word of every single person is their own name. If you remember the name and a fact or two about everyone you meet you can go far with making new friends.

My game plan was easy; keep track of everyone's names and likes and pet peeves in a handy notebook.

How would this tactic get me a boyfriend? No idea. But if I wanted a cool guy, I had to be cool, too. Right?

There I was at fifteen, strolling through the hallways between classes, waving hello and calling out to everyone by their name. Asking about their sports, pets, family, and significant others.

It was amazing how quickly I zoomed up the high school hierarchy. I wasn't popular like Bridget who was a legit star. I was more of an ambassador. Teachers and the principal recognized my connection to the students and asked me to take on leadership roles.

While steering a coalition on diversity I met Ivandro. He'd migrated to Maine with his family along with other families from Angola.

When I heard about their difficult, life-threatening series of border crossings, I realized there was a world of pain out there.

Ivandro was tall, dark, handsome, intensely angry at the world, with a body Magic Mike dancers would cry for, and full of disdain for authority, but struggling to fit in anyway.

He spoke only Portuguese when we met.

As I tutored him in English, I began learning how to speak Portuguese. I discovered my love for languages and their ability to connect people.

Within a week, I was in love with Ivandro. He was better than the TV guys. He was real.

More importantly, he liked me back. Not that he had much of a choice. I was the only person he could communicate with a for a while.

I lived for his kisses at my locker, holding hands on the bus, the beach bonfire parties, and cliff walks by the lighthouse.

The world sparkled and glowed. Of course, I ignored the red flags. Or rather, I explained them away.

When he was moody and snapped at me, I chalked it up to anxiety over his immigration status.

When he drank too much and got loud, I said he was expressing his true emotions at the world that had given him a cold shoulder.

When he ignored my text messages, but I could see him flirting with other girls, I told myself not to be so clingy.

What did I expect if I wanted the hot guy? The cool dude. The bad boy.

By Christmas, Ivandro was out of my life. Not because he left Maine.

He'd decided that relationships weren't his jam.

That's exactly how he phrased it. "You're sweet, Corrine, but relationships aren't my jam."

Needless to say, I'd taught him enough English to provide him with his parting words to me.

By New Year's Eve, he was dating the head cheerleader. Only fitting since he'd moved up to captain of the soccer team with international scouts checking him out.

But he left me with a solid precedent. I began falling into one angsty relationship after another. Their end dates were always sooner than my lunchtime yogurt expiration dates.

The boys were different. Some played sports, some played video games, and some played around.

But the one common denominator was that the connections were dramatic, intense, heart-racing, and unfulfilling.

Like chaos and uncertainty represented my end game. Love had to be rocky and play itself out.

This love junkie dating cycle went on through high school and into college.

Which is why my year abroad is my chance to reinvent myself *again*.

This time I am older, wiser and I can't *fall* in love. Like a top spinning across the floor and tipping over when it's lost its momentum.

Love is life and death for me.

But I can't take any more chances with my heart. Or my mental and physical health.

This time around, love will have to prove itself in more ways than one.

I'm not falling for the bad boy again.

I'm not falling for Salvador Torres.

Chapter Nineteen

"Don't do it, you bad boy!" I shake a finger at the puppy. His paws grip the edge of my covers.

He's determined to drag the entire bedding onto the floor with him since I won't let the scoundrel on the bed with me.

He licks my hand as I reach down to yank the sheets back up.

"I'm not playing tug of war with you, mister. I already bathed you and fed you the leftovers that I was planning to eat tonight. Now you want my bed too?"

He leaps into the air and yelps loudly. I don't know dogs at all but that is a clear call to action. As in, *come play with me*.

"Shush!" I waggle my finger again. This time more sternly.

He watches my finger go up and down, his head and tail moving in time with my finger.

I choke back a laugh.

He leaps at my finger and almost gets it before I pull it away just in time.

"Oh, you're a comedian."

Arf!

I put my finger to my lips and motion with my hand to keep the noise down.

"Which part of 'you're only here for one night so don't make noise' do you not get?"

I yawn and slide my reading glasses off my face.

"How did I get roped into babysitting you, huh?"

Arf! He sits back on his chubby legs eyeing me as if I have all the answers.

"Look, tomorrow we'll take you to a nice place where they'll find you a good home with children and maybe other pets, okay?"

He tilts his head as if he's understanding my words.

We stare at each other.

For a furry little thing, he's got intense soulful brown eyes. As if he sees right through me.

He probably knows that my heart is racing at the idea of seeing Salvador Torres again tomorrow.

Hours ago, when the sky was darkening and Izzy was still fast asleep on his lap, I'd invited Salvador to bring her upstairs until she awoke.

Night was coming and the air had taken a turn from cool to chilly.

"I'll call for a car," he said. "But thank you."

As he closed off the call, I'd looked at him in alarm. "What are we going to do with this puppy? We can't leave him here in the garden."

The little fur ball had whimpered in his sleep. Like he knew we were planning his fate.

Salvador already had the answer. "Can you keep him for one night? I'll come by tomorrow morning. We can take him to a good animal shelter where they'll find him a home. If I take him home tonight, Izzy will never let him leave. And that's a commitment I can't make right now."

He'd glanced down at the sleeping dog. "He's cute though."

I agreed. "Someone will want him."

What does he mean he can't commit? To a dog? Imagine a woman! No, don't go there, Corrine. You're not interested in him remember?

Now I eye the dog warily on the floor by my bed. "I can't keep you either. Cute as you may be."

I think about the busy schedule I have now that I'll be tutoring Izzy in English several days a week. Salvador didn't tell me why it was so important that she learn English as quickly as possible.

I have classes at the university four days a week. Then afternoon and evening meet-ups with the up-and-coming young writers of Portugal. Many of them live in Porto due to Porto's long and impressive literary history.

Even J.K. Rowling lived in Porto and taught English here. Many of Porto's landscapes and architecture inspired the settings in her Harry Potter books.

I want to connect with these writers. Be a part of their inner circle so they will trust me to translate their novels.

Most people don't realize how deeply connected a translator must be to the writer to understand the feelings of the book, not just the words.

If I could be half as talented as Margaret Jull Costa, an award-winning translator, I'd be very happy.

While dating Ivandro, so much of our communication got lost in translation.

It's not just words that are different, the feelings behind them and how you express the words mean more.

Being an English translator of Spanish and Portuguese books is what I have wanted to do since I met Ivandro.

So, even though it didn't work out, and heck we were fifteen years old, I found my calling.

"This goes to show, that if you step outside your box, you may find your world."

Arf!

"Oh, no," I groan and collapse into the sheets. "I didn't just say that!" I speak to the puppy who's staring intently at me.

Arf! He grabs the edge of the covers again and shakes his head hard like he's fighting a dragon.

"No!"

I sigh and pull up the covers so they don't hang down and tempt this little monster again.

My mind runs over the day. The way Salvador teased me. How he was so tender with his daughter.

That man . . . ohhh!

He's got the whole protective vibe going, but not in an off-putting macho way.

It's natural, in an *I'm here for you and don't argue with it* kind of way.

But I can't let myself trust that vibe. I've had bad instincts when it comes to men who walk, talk, smell, and look like him. As if they were warriors or knights in their past lives.

I'm committed to dating artistic, sensitive, smart book lovers and even writers. That would be ideal. A sexy writer with a soul to share.

Like . . . *hmmm* . . . well, no one comes to mind.

But I've put it out there in the Universe. I want a man who stimulates my brain. One who fires up my intellect and challenges me mentally.

Not a guy whose muscles ripple through his clothing like one of the Hemsworth brothers.

And not a man whose kisses I know I'll dream about tonight.

Oh boy!

The puppy whimpers with me.

"We're in trouble, dog."

Chapter Twenty

I woke up expecting to see a disaster in my apartment. Instead, the puppy is sleeping tangled in the towel I'd placed on the floor, and everything looks in place.

Still, I tiptoe around looking into corners in case he made any messes I must clean up.

"Wow! I can't call you a bad boy anymore. You're an angel."

I look down to find him at my heels. His pink tongue hangs out and I swear he looks excited to see me. "Let's go outside. I'm sure you need a walk."

His tail wags back and forth in a furry arc.

Before I fell asleep last night, I'd googled how to care for puppies, so I'd know what to do on this one day we have together.

I learned that walks are essential, which is fine with me. I scheduled a fifteen-minute walk before eating breakfast at home.

The rest of my calendar is clear for me to go with Salvador to take the puppy to the shelter where they will find him a home. My one class today is after lunch.

"Come on, you."

I throw on sweats and tuck him under one arm.

I'd made a leash out of a belt last night to prepare for our morning walk. The buckle of my sparkly silver belt fits snugly under his chin. I wrap the end of the belt around one wrist.

We established he's a boy dog last night. I hope he's male enough to sport a pretty collar.

As I step into the hallway and get ready to hoof it fast down the stairs, a voice calls out to me.

"Woo hoo!"

I glance over my shoulder with a smile. "Hey Sylvia, can we catch up in a bit? I have to run."

She eyes the squirming bundle under my arm. "Oh, who's that?"

I put a finger to my lips. "He's leaving today. It was an emergency."

She nods. "Mighty cute though."

Arf! The puppy seems to agree.

"I gotta go, I don't want him having any accidents on me."

"Okay, stop by when you can."

I wave and scurry down the steps.

As soon as we step out the front door, I set him on the ground and steer him to the garden in front.

"Do your business fast," I hiss. I'm not sure if pets are allowed. But in case they aren't, I don't want to be kicked out of my apartment for breaking any landlord/tenant rules.

The puppy stares at the garden like he's searching for Izzy.

I walk over to the same bench we'd sat on yesterday. "They're gone, buddy."

He doesn't listen to me. He leaps onto a stick and does some kind of wrestling move the Rock would be proud of.

"Stop rolling around. I don't have all day."

I sweet-talk him into following me to a tree.

"This is where dogs do their business right?"

I shake out the plastic zip lock baggy I found under my sink ready to do my part.

He eyes me. I eye him back.

"Fine." I turn around and look away. Maybe he wants privacy.

"What kind of stray dog are you anyway? You act like you're royalty who needs special treatment."

Arf! Arf!

I giggle. "Are you answering me back?"

An hour later, I'm in the front seat of Salvador's luxurious European car.

I am dressed in my oldest, softest jeans and a University of Porto sweatshirt knowing we'd be dealing with the dog.

Salvador looks magnificent.

A black turtleneck, blue slacks, a leather blazer, and polished wing-tip shoes. My immediate thought is *Whoa!*

But that's the old Corrine.

The new reinventing herself Corrine, merely nods hello and slides into the seat without a word.

After exchanging some small talk about how the puppy behaved last night, he asks, "What do you have planned today? After we drop him off?"

The puppy is sleeping in a box on the floor by my feet. Hearing Salvador say, *"Drop him off,"* in such a casual manner makes my stomach clench.

I eyeball the pup. I'm not getting attached to you, little monster, I say in my head.

"Hello, Corrine?"

I snap my head up. "Oh, I'm busy. I have a class. Then I'm

meeting with some writers at . . .." My brain scrambles to remember where the writers' group is meeting today.

Salvador raises a perfect eyebrow at me. "It's a secret?"

I ignore his question. Mostly because I have no clue without looking at my schedule, which is in my bag by the puppy's box.

"I hope they find him a good home." My toe touches the edge of the box. A weird choking feeling fills my throat. Making it hard to swallow.

"What are you doing after . . . this?" I force myself to focus on Salvador and stop staring at the brown furball in the box.

"Going to *Sangria Nights*."

"Ah! Work."

"Fun work."

"All your work is fun," I say. "Playing football. And running a bar."

"Don't be jealous."

"I'm not," I scoff. "I don't want to run around a field and toss drinks in the air."

He laughs. "Who says we toss drinks in the air?"

"Every bar movie I've ever seen."

"What do *you* prefer? A delicious sangria or listening to pseudo-intellectuals ramble on about the modern novel?"

"They're not pseudo-intellectuals. As if you would know anything about the modern novel."

He scrunches up his forehead and smiles devilishly at me. "It comes with owning a bar. I hear it all. Consider the bar to be my university. You'd be surprised how many intellectuals drink alcohol."

"Oh, I know," I sigh. "The smarter they are, the more they drink."

He laughs aloud. "As long as they're having a good time at *Sangria Nights*, I'm glad. We want everyone to enjoy themselves. We don't discriminate. We let in smart people, too."

He eyes me up and down. "Want to come?"

"Where to? Your bar? In the middle of the day?"

He slaps the steering wheel. "We're not going to drink. I want to show it to you. So you can see what it's like."

"As long as that's all. I'm wearing my doggie armor." I run my hand up and down my torso.

He glances at me as he swings the car into a graveled parking lot while he says, "You look beautiful."

Salvador slides the vehicle into a parking space.

The puppy sticks up his head and barks.

I eye the gray building. I read up on the facility before we left my apartment. It is highly rated. But now that I'm here, I don't like it one bit.

"Are you sure this place will find him a good home?"

"My PA called around. It's the best."

"Okay," I say reluctantly as I open my car door. Before I can stand up the puppy climbs out of the box and leaps from the car.

"Come back here!" I shout.

He trots into the open door of the building as if he's home.

"You didn't say goodbye." I wail.

Chapter Twenty-One

I didn't think I'd cry. In fact, I'd have bet money I wouldn't cry when we left the animal shelter.

But tears are streaming down my face as if I just said goodbye to a childhood pet.

"I thought this might happen." Salvador swings the car over to the side and stops. He wraps a strong arm around my body and slides me over to his seat.

The car is obscenely huge, so there's lots of space.

But still, sitting on Salvador's lap is a no-no for many reasons: 1) he's my new boss, 2) he's a football player and probably does this kind of thing all the time, and 3) he may still be with his baby mama — that fact has not been ascertained.

And last, but what *should* be first, I am a strong, independent woman who does not need to cry on a man's shoulder!

Meanwhile, my tears won't stop. "I miss that annoying bad boy already!"

Salvador rubs circles on my back. His thumb slides up to my bare skin by my neck and I shiver. "It's okay. I'll be your bad boy."

I sniff and lean back to gaze into his eyes. If he only knew that is the worst thing that he could say to make me feel better.

"I don't need a bad boy like you. I just miss the puppy."

Salvador sniffs loudly. "Consider my feelings officially hurt."

I drop my head into that space between his shoulder and neck, where his clavicles resemble those of a Hercules statue.

"I'll need a minute," I say staunchly.

His hold tightens around me. "Take as long as you need. I am here and I'm not going anywhere."

I sigh. He sounds perfect. But nobody is. "Why can't you be a normal guy? One who would say, 'Get a grip. It's a dog, not a person.'"

A soft snort escapes him. "Normal is overrated, my dear. Get some friends who are unique and special like me."

"I plan to."

He squeezes me. "Not a pseudo-intellectual who doesn't know his book from his butthole though."

"Oh my god! You didn't."

He laughs. "Did I get your mind off the puppy?"

I smack his chest. "No . . . maybe. But you shocked me."

He throws me a winning smile, full face with crinkly eyes and all. I melt a bit. Why'd he have to be so darn handsome?

"By the way, how old are you?" I ask.

He gently shifts me over to my side of the car. I feel suddenly bereft as if he's taken away my personal security blanket.

"Old enough."

"God, I hate that answer."

He chuckles. "Google me, then."

I eye him wickedly. "I did a little, but I stopped. I don't think it's fair that I would know everything about you, and you know nothing about me."

His hands drop from the steering wheel. He tilts his head and stares at me like I'm something he's never seen before.

"What?" I ask.

"This right here is why I adore you."

"What?" I'm confused. "You adore me, why?"

"Because you're not like anyone else. You don't care about my status or my money or my . . . *anything*."

If he only knew how hard I concentrated to not want his kisses and what else went with them.

His eyes are a clear sparkly gray like a silver dress you'd wear on New Year's Eve.

"I care . . . *a bit*."

"People are eager to research me from top to bottom, even checking my Net Worth online."

"Ouch! That must be hard." I hold his hand. "No privacy at all."

"None. I have days when the paparazzi are out, and I prepare for them mentally. And even physically. But then days like today, I drive this understated car. Not my red sports car, so they'll leave me alone."

I pull my hand out of his grip and wave it in the air. "So, me and the bad boy get the *boring* car?"

A big smile lights up his face as he wheels the boring car back onto the road. "We can go get my other one right now!"

I glance around the comfortable luxury vehicle. "Nah, I'm okay with this. It'll do."

He laughs. "First time anyone ever said that about a Maybach."

"Never heard of it. Can't be that special."

His hoot of a laugh helps ease the pain of leaving the puppy behind.

Why do I feel as if I'm abandoning him? He waved his tail at me when I was leaving. Although his little yelps of goodbye sounded sad to my ears.

I'm going to be positive and hope he finds himself a perfect new home.

Chapter Twenty-Two

If I wanted to own and operate my own restaurant and bar, it would look exactly like *Sangria Nights*.

Giant polished wooden doors with etched grape leaves adorning the edges lead the way inside *Sangria Nights*.

The establishment sits one level up from the edge of the riverbank. A patio is flooded with sunshine and juts out over the river. From inside and outside you have a perfect view of the bridge and the boats chugging up and down the waterway.

"Almost everything in the restaurant is refurbished from old Quintas up the Douro River valley." Salvador slides a hand across the wood of the door and looks at me with a shy smile.

The way he's caressing the door makes my heart shimmy inside my chest. The man has giant hands. Imagine them caressing *my* body.

Get your mind out of the gutter, Corrine.

"We wanted it to be authentic. We canvassed all the old farms and vineyards looking for stuff we could use here." He's watching my face as if waiting for a reaction.

Other than getting swept up in Salvador's masculinity, which seeps from his pores the way sweat emanates from most people, I'm distracted by a queasy feeling in the pit of my stomach.

Like I want to throw up.

Except I haven't eaten anything since the puppy and I shared toast this morning.

I bite my lip to stop asking Salvador how he thinks the puppy is doing. It's not as if he'd know the answer.

I'm itching to call the animal shelter and ask them if he's playing with the toy I made from an old sock. Or sleeping in a round furry ball.

"Are you hungry, Corrine?" Salvador gently maneuvers my body inside the cool timber-roofed bar area.

Upbeat pop music explodes from speakers concealed around the space.

It's almost 2 p.m. and I expected the restaurant to be empty, but the place is hopping with a rowdy after-lunchtime crowd.

Based on the number of cameras and selfie-sticks on the table, along with wide-brimmed hats, I'd say *Sangria Nights* is a mecca for every tourist in Porto.

"Wow! All of this is you?" My eyes don't know where to land first. The polished wooden bar with a counter that looks as big as a floating raft.

Cute tables decorated with Porto's iconic cotton tablecloths featuring traditional motifs and lovers' quotes.

"I love those tablecloths," I exclaim. "I can sit here and read them all day."

He laughs. "Feel free to translate them aloud in English to the tourists. They're always asking us what the sayings mean."

"It'll cost you."

"You're hired."

I grab a seat at the bar. "Get me a pen and paper and I'll write out a list of translations and you can laminate and leave them on the tables, like menus. That way your guests can learn about your culture while they eat."

Salvador leans his back against the bar. His eyes open wide as he considers my idea. "How come I never thought of that."

I smile weakly, my stomach roiling for unknown reasons. "You can't think of everything. This place is stunning."

A rush of blood floods his face. Salvador Torres is *blushing*? I catch the same look in his eyes that I saw after his epic game in Athens where he'd scored two goals.

Like he wants *my* praise. It gives me an intoxicating feeling of power. That he could *want* my praise, much less need it.

I'd tease him about it if I weren't distracted by the queasy feeling in the pit of my stomach.

"Are you hungry?" Salvador asks again, signaling for the bartender to come over.

"He looks very busy," I whisper. I grip my stomach again. What is wrong with me?

Salvador catches my movement and frowns. "When was the last time you ate? Is it hunger pangs?"

His intense stare is overpowering. I have never had anyone look at me like this. Or ask me so intently if I was okay.

I am used to being on my own. Not having all this attention. Other than my therapist, I've never confessed I am in pain about anything. That isn't me.

I was diagnosed as a "stoic patient." I didn't even know that was a thing when I was fourteen and first went to see a therapist to discuss my eating disorder.

I kept saying I was fine. Nothing is wrong. Even though I knew that binge eating and throwing up was not fine. Not one bit.

Nor was getting entangled with guys I chose for all the wrong reasons.

I still haven't evolved enough to admit pain to anyone. Not even my sisters. I'm not about to tell Salvador I feel like throwing up. It's beyond embarrassing.

"Excuse me," I slide off my bar seat. "Where're your restrooms?"

He points me in the direction of a side hallway. Inside the stall, I stare at the water in the toilet.

I flip down the lid and sit down on the closed toilet seat.

I pull out my phone and dial my therapist. I check the time. It's a decent hour to call her. She answers after a few rings.

"It's been a while, Corrine. How are you?"

Her voice sounds the same as when I sat across from her every week for three years.

"I'm not sure," I say honestly. "I feel queasy. But not from eating. It feels like . . .."

"Like?"

I swallow hard. "Like sadness. It hit me out of the blue."

"Have you had a recent loss of any kind?"

"I moved to Portugal. But you knew that."

"Right. Are you missing your family?"

I shake my head. "No, I talk to them a lot. And I saw Bridget a month ago in Greece."

"Hmmm. Are you dating anyone?"

I shake my head vigorously. My hair slides over my shoulder and I toss it back. "No one." That's not a lie. Salvador and I are not dating.

The door to the restroom opens and voices filter in. Young women giggle. I hear the words, "Salvador Torres."

"I can't talk here," I whisper.

"Corrine, call me this evening. I have a free hour at five my time."

"Okay, thanks, Ms. Kepler."

"It's Katrina," she chuckles. "I'm here for you Corrine. But I think we should find you someone in Porto. In case I'm not available."

I mumble, "Okay." Then hang up.

Chapter Twenty-Three

After the women leave the restroom, I exit the stall and stand in front of the mirror washing my hands.

My usual bright brown eyes appear hollow. My stomach feels like marbles are rolling around in it.

I inhale deeply and let out my breath slowly, following lessons I've learned on self-calming.

When I push open the bathroom door, I run smack into Salvador. His arms are crossed over his chest, a grim look on his face.

Now I know why the women were talking about him.

Salvador's lips flatten without smiling. His eyes dig into me with an emotion so unexpected I can't name it.

"Why are you looking at me like that?"

"Why are you running and hiding out in the bathroom?"

I stare back at his stormy gray eyes. "Are you for real?"

"I am. I don't play games."

I could smirk and say you get *paid* to play games, but I don't dare.

"What's your deal? Why are you following me?" I stride down the corridor and back into the wide-open restaurant. I slide into my seat at the bar.

He follows without replying. Then brings forward a bowl of soup, a plate of the most delicious fresh-baked bread, and a bowl of something that looks like pudding topped with fresh berries.

It all smells and looks exactly like what I would order for myself. I raise an eyebrow at him. "How'd you know I'd like this?"

He shrugs. The worried expression still flickering in his eyes.

"We ate at the party in Athens, remember? You said you loved soup and pudding. Food for people who don't chew."

I glare at him. "I chew." I take a bite of the bread and a spoonful of the rich beef stew. "This is delicious," I admit. "Thank you."

He settles into the seat next to me.

"Aren't you going to eat, too?"

The bartender brings over a tall glass of a greenish shake and slides it toward Salvador.

"I'm on a diet," he says.

I cover my mouth so my laugh doesn't escape.

"I thought you Americans were more respectful of people's dietary needs."

I suck in my cheeks to stop the smile. "We are. I'm sorry. Good luck with that *diet*." I grimace at the drink he's ingesting with green bits floating around in it.

"So." He turns and stares at me.

I swallow my spoonful of stew and dip my bread in it swirling up some rich broth. My stomach isn't wobbling around like before. Maybe I was just hungry.

"So what?" I counter.

A loud burst of laughter comes from a table against the wall.

College-aged kids are clicking glasses of sangria and singing along to songs on the overhead speakers.

"Why'd you disappear into the bathroom to call someone? You have a big secret you can't tell me? Are you sick?"

"What?"

"I didn't stutter."

I can't believe the audacity of this man.

I stare into his eyes which are turning darker by the second. He does not blink.

I try to hold his stare, but my eyes slide away to the bar top.

Face it, Corrine, he's not the kind of guy you need or want in your life. You want a sensitive, sweet guy. One who would respect your privacy. And read the same kinds of books. Or at least read!

Salvador and I have nothing in common. Especially seeing this side of him, which appears possessive.

"I'm sorry. I must go." I jump off the stool and search in my bag for my wallet.

As I pull it out, Salvador stands up. "Stop it. You're not paying for this food. And I'm sorry if you don't like my concern. You looked ill."

My breath is coming so fast and furious I can't feel my hands. Or the bills I'm trying to pull out. How does he know? No one ever knew when I felt anything other than in control.

I finally get one out and slide it across the counter toward the bartender. "Thanks," I mutter.

"Corrine, stop," Salvador is large, but he's never seen me cornered. I push past him like he's a blow-up toy.

"Don't follow me," I growl.

I hurry down the steps and towards the university. I knew it was a mistake hanging out with him.

An image of how gentle and caring he was in his car when I was crying over the puppy flashes through my mind.

That was probably an anomaly. The real Salvador Torres is a bundle of contradictions, mysteries, and lord knows what else.

I stomp toward my classroom. I'm early but I'll wait outside and read.

I bite the inside of my cheek to stop any wayward tears that could appear. Because thoughts swirl around my head twofold.

What am I going to do about the job I need if I'm not speaking to Salvador?

How is the puppy doing on his first day at the Animal Rescue shelter?

Chapter Twenty-Four

I may not be able to do anything about the puppy, but I can put out feelers for another job.

While I wait for class to start, I search online classified ads for any type of part-time job. Translating texts or tutoring would be ideal.

But at this point, I'd take a sales job. Bookstore, clothing store, doesn't matter.

I'd have to work longer hours. That would cut into my time socializing with the *Porto Writers & Poets Club* and trying to connect with its members.

The first meet-up I attended last week had a few hiccups.

I speak Portuguese, the language everyone was speaking. I understood the nuances of their discussions. I've read many of the books they were discussing.

Yet, I couldn't help but feel as if I was trying to infiltrate an exclusive club. One that didn't see me as an asset. As if I had to prove myself.

But how do you prove yourself to a book club? Read more?

I recall Salvador saying they were pseudo-intellectuals.

Of course, to a professional athlete, a bunch of writers may seem like intellectual snobs, but they shouldn't seem like that to me. I'm one of them. They just don't know it yet.

This is why I've been doing my own translation of their Nobel Prize-winning author, Jose Saragamo. To show them I can handle their literary treasures. And by extension, their own up-and-coming works.

The next meeting is this evening at a cafe near the university. I'm going to chill, play it cool, and let them get to know me on their own terms. Whatever those are.

This way they'll feel comfortable choosing me to translate their stories. I hope. It's the entire reason for my being in Porto.

This beautiful city is the hub of the writers' movers and shakers of Portugal.

By the time the professor opens the classroom door and starts our class on Portuguese culture, a requisite for my year abroad program, and my favorite class, I've emailed a bunch of resumes.

I've also created a list of my attributes that I can share with the writers and poets at the meet-up later.

Like being a diverse voice to add an additional level of understanding to their texts.

Like living close to Boston where I have access to many collegiate libraries and resources for help with translating their books.

Most of all, I have life experiences that help me empathize with their characters and themes.

A lot of these writers are diving into the loss of humanity with the rise of Artificial Intelligence. I understand loss well. Maybe better than most my age.

Translators are creative interpreters of a writer's work, so whatever emotion a writer brings to his work, the translator must double that.

I want them to see I can elevate their potential literary classics.

Unfortunately, I feel as if I'm waiting to be chosen at a dodgeball game in the high school gym and no one wants the skinny, short girl on their team.

"That's cute. Is that your dog?"

A young man with a Brazilian accent is leaning across our shared desk pointing at my notebook.

"What?" I look at where he's pointing.

I've doodled thumbnail drawings of the puppy. His little furry face. His head tilt. Without realizing it.

"No, he isn't," I say. I smile politely.

The guy nods.

"I wish he was," I whisper.

He smiles. "I'm Carlos. I didn't mean to distract you."

I whisper my name then say, "I should be paying attention."

He grins. "You and me both."

I drop my pen and look to the front of the classroom.

The professor is discussing a tragic time in Porto's history. The death of thousands of people in the Douro River in the early 19th century during the Peninsular War.

"That's genocide," Carlos says in a shocked voice.

I nod numbly.

As I listen to my professor discuss how this event affected the culture of the people, I remember how tragedy felt in my own life. Like a monster you cannot control. Or subdue.

I'm feeling a bit of that monster encroaching now. But I'm not sure what I am sad about.

Is it the war that happened not far from here?

Is it the separation I'm feeling from a puppy that I only knew for one day?

Or is it the loss of Salvador Torres, whom I shouldn't miss in the first place?

Chapter Twenty-Five

As class wraps up, Carlos asks if I want to grab a coffee to discuss a term paper we're scheduled to turn in next week.

"I would love to," I say sincerely. "But I'm heading to the meet-up for the *Porto Writers and Poets Club*."

Carlos raises his eyebrows like he's impressed. "You're a writer?"

I shake my head. "A translator. Of novels. That's my plan anyway."

"Sharing knowledge across cultures and countries, I see," he smiles.

"Yes, you get it! Do you want to come? It's a cafe so we can still drink coffee."

He responds by grabbing his backpack and signaling for us to go.

I grab my stuff and shove it into my backpack. "Cool." I feel much lighter heading over with a companion.

We chat amiably about the small town in Brazil where he was born. "It's so tiny the main street is in another town," he says, using his hands to show me how the street cut through the towns.

"You're a man of two worlds."

He nods. "Don't you think everyone is a person of two worlds? Their internal world *and* their external world? In my case, it was literal as well as figurative."

Carlos has a point.

"What about you?" he asks. "Are you a woman of two worlds?"

"I'd say more like three worlds. My American world. My Portuguese world. And . . . my internal world." As I say it aloud, I realize how true it is.

"Do you find it difficult navigating between your two external worlds?"

Before I can think about that, the door to the cafe swings open. Boisterous students step out laughing and Carlos holds open the door for me to enter.

The cafe is buzzing with noise. People talking, a low hum of music, and the very loud grinding of coffee beans by the espresso machine.

The blue-tiled walls feature wheat fields and flowers from the countryside. It never ceases to amaze me how beautiful the architecture is in this lively city.

Not to mention the aroma of sauteed buttery sandwiches and sweet pastries emanating from behind the counters.

I glance around at the groups of students. I notice the writers and poets sprawled across two sofas and a bunch of armchairs like they own one-half of the room.

"They don't look intimidating at all," I mutter.

For the record, I don't get intimidated easily. But this is my future profession. I am concerned about making a good impression.

Carlos hears me because he chuckles. "No one attacks harder than a writer with a cause."

I square my shoulders. "You're right. Let's hope there's no need for any attacking today."

"If there is, I got your back, as they say in America."

"Thanks, my loyal soldier in arms. Let's proceed."

We order coffee and I ask for a pastry to go with mine. I haven't eaten anything but toast with the puppy and a spoonful of stew and bread with Salvador. All of which feels like days ago instead of hours.

Carlos signals to the cashier that he would like the same pastry. "Sugar and spice and everything nice."

"Not that nice. What's our plan?"

He shrugs. "Humor is the hidden sword of the cleverest opponent. I say we kill them with jokes."

"Wow!" I stop and stare at my comrade. "You're cute *and* smart."

He blushes. "I should be insulted. Imagine if I said that to you."

My turn to blush. "I'm sorry. That was a bit . . .."

"Sexist?"

"I was going to say rude."

"So, sexist *and* rude."

I bark out a laugh. "Consider me corrected."

The writers' and poets' eyes are on us as we walk toward their corner balancing coffees and pastries.

With feisty Carlos along for the ride, I feel emboldened. I'm not only making a new friend, but I'm also forging an alliance.

I don't know if it's because they have changed their perception of me since last week, which doesn't seem likely, or if tall, dark, handsome Carlos, a native Portuguese speaker, is a bridge to their world.

This time, the club members say "olá" and smile at me.

I settle into an empty seat with Carlos sitting cross-legged at my feet.

For every comment on life or observation on literature one of them makes, Carlos interjects a funny comeback.

Soon, we're all laughing so much that we forget to discuss the books at hand.

I'm almost able to put Salvador Torres and a cute furry puppy out of my mind.

But not quite.

Chapter Twenty-Six

"I think that was a very successful evening," Carlos says as he walks with me down the hills of Porto toward the river. "We must do this again."

"You must promise not to crack us all up with your jokes. We won't accomplish anything."

"On the contrary," he says. "We accomplished exactly what needed to get done today. You are now an official member of the club.

I smile. "Thanks to you."

"I'm happy to help. It's for the cause."

I step carefully as we meander across cobblestones and stroll down my favorite *Rua das Flores*. If Salvador was walking with me, I have no doubt he'd take hold of my arm and guide me safely down the slippery street.

But he's not here. And that's a good thing, right?

I'm walking with an intelligent, book-smart, handsome guy who managed to break down barriers to an exclusive intellectual group without having fame or fortune.

Carlos is exactly the kind of guy I want to date. I wonder if he lives near me or if I'll have to wait until class to see him again.

As if he's reading my mind, he stops at the bottom of the hill.

"I go that way." He points in the opposite direction to my apartment. "You?"

I point in my direction.

He nods. "Well, I had a lot of fun. Thank you for inviting me to join you. Can we do this again?"

"Attend a meeting?"

He shakes his head. His fade is cut tight. His dark skin glistens under the streetlamps. He looks like a Black Panther character but with glasses and a backpack.

"No, I'd like to ask you out on a real date." His eyes are serious. "May I have your phone number?"

"Oh." I blink under the streetlamps. "Uh-huh," I say.

What's wrong with you girl? Answer the man properly.

I clear my throat. "Yes. I would love that." I put my number in his phone.

His face breaks into a winning smile. "Great. I'll text you."

I nod. "Great."

We say goodbye and I head in my direction, kicking at pebbles as I stroll along the promenade.

I accomplished so much this evening.

Why is my stomach tied up in knots? I'm not doing anything wrong. I'm not being unfaithful. I owe Salvador nothing.

Nothing!

As I near my apartment, I see a car under the lights outside the gate. A car that looks like a fancy European luxury brand. With a name I do not know.

My feet pick up speed. I'm almost running.

Slow down, Corrine. He is not here for you.

Right, tell that to my feet and my heart and my stomach, which is suddenly leaping like a ballet dancer in mid-twirl.

Chapter Twenty-Seven

"Where the heck have you been? It's late." He makes a production of looking at his watch.

"What is your problem?" All the glee at seeing Salvador again flies right out of my body.

"This is my problem! We've been waiting here for hours!" Salvador points to a basket on the front seat of his car.

"Ahhhh!" I scream aloud with joy. I slap a hand over my mouth. Salvador pulls my hand away.

"Let me enjoy the moment," he growls.

"How did you know?" My eyes dart between him and the puppy.

The intensity in his eyes pierces my soul. Like he sees to my inner demons.

But obviously, that's my imagination. No one knows about those except my therapist.

I clasp my hands together. "This is the best thing anyone's ever done for me. But I can't keep him," I say regretfully.

"Yes, you can. I'll explain later. But you and me . . ." He wags his finger between us. "We're his parents now."

"We are?"

"No more questions, just thank me properly." He grins broadly.

I throw myself onto Salvador. He catches me with one large hand and cradles me like I'm the most precious thing in the world.

All the anxiety of my day seeps out of me in a whoosh.

"I'm sorry, baby," Salvador mumbles in my hair.

I'm not sure what he's saying sorry about. But at this moment all I want is to close my eyes tightly and lean into this man.

How can I go from feeling out of sorts all day to feeling completely right just by seeing him? Or maybe it's the puppy.

I twist around in Salvador's heavily muscled arms to gaze at the puppy snoring in a woven basket with chocolate brown velvet bedding. It looks as fancy as the car.

"We should be quiet. He looks so peaceful."

"I'm not the one screaming." He laughs happily. I hear relief in his voice.

I turn and bury my face in his chest again. "I was worried about him. I even missed him."

My words are muffled but Salvador seems to understand. He pulls me closer. Wraps both arms around me and runs his hands up and down my back.

"I think he missed us, too."

I lean back a little so I can see his eyes. They're gray and calm and gentle now, like the sea after a storm.

"How do you know he missed us?"

"I just know," he says abruptly, pulling me back to fit under his chin. As if he wants to inhale my essence. My blood, bones, and cells. Every part of me.

I've never experienced this before. The feeling that someone could want me so much they literally want to breathe me in.

"You're like the big bad wolf in Little Red Riding Hood, aren't you?"

"What?" he chortles. But doesn't release his grip.

"Yes, you want to devour me."

He says somberly, "I'm not the wolf. But I'll protect you from the wolf. Or *wolves*."

I press my body closer. My softness yields to his hard maleness. I slide my arms under his leather jacket and around his waist.

"Maybe *I'm* the wolf," I mumble, feeling the urge to stay where I am absorbing his heat like a drug I need without dosage limitations.

After a few minutes, I pull myself together.

"Where's Izzy?" I ask, peering up at him from under my lashes.

"At home. My aunt lives with us. She's our caretaker. Treats me and Izzy like we're her kids."

"That's wonderful." I swallow. "I think I may be addicted to the puppy," I say. "Today felt like it was missing something important."

"Yes, *me*." He rubs circles on my back. "Just like I missed you. For over a month."

His self-assurance is a bit unnerving.

"How do you *know* you like me?"

"Because you're for me."

"Meaning?"

"You are mine. I knew it the moment you smiled up at me and invited me to sit next to you on the plane. And just now when you're concerned about my daughter you just met. And your attachment to an innocent puppy. You are the girl I want in my life. Can we talk about this later, please."

He opens the car door and gathers the basket in his arms. "Let's get our little devil upstairs before he wakes up? And we need to give him a name. You can't keep calling him 'bad boy.'"

"No, wait. You can't go around telling women they're yours. Like a caveman. You realize we're in the 21st century?"

"I totally agree, darling. I don't tell women. Only you."

I poof out a bubble of disgust. "You're just cocky."

"And you love it."

"That remains to be seen."

As Salvador carries the basket with the puppy still asleep in it across the sidewalk and through the garden gate, I walk behind them glancing left and right like I'm the security detail.

Chapter Twenty-Eight

"What is my landlord going to say?" I whisper anxiously. "I might get kicked out. Although I'm willing to take the risk."

I tiptoe behind Salvador as we traverse the grounds.

It's true. I'd give up being able to look at the Dom Luís I bridge if it meant I could keep the furry, exasperating bundle in Salvador's arms.

"I handled it. The puppy is fine here. You're fine here. Until." Salvador strides up the stairs without once glancing around.

I follow on silent feet, hoping not to get caught. *Until what?* I wonder.

Once we're safely inside my apartment, I lock the door.

Salvador has placed the basket on the floor next to my bed and I peer into it.

"I hope he likes sleeping next to me."

"He gets to sleep with you before I do, huh?" Salvador snorts.

I raise my eyebrows at him. "If *ever*."

"That's a *when* not an *if*, my dear." He bends down and kisses the tip of my nose. "I love how you need convincing."

I suck my teeth.

Before I can say another word, Salvador Torres picks me up

and presses my head back trailing a line of hot steamy kisses down my throat.

Heat floods my belly. Shivers of excitement thrill down my spine.

I've gripped his arms to hold on and I feel his biceps tensing under my fingertips like they're just waiting to be unleashed from his shirt.

This man is a walking stick of dynamite. I'd better watch out.

He releases me but one of his arms holds me up so I don't completely hit the floor like a sack of potatoes.

I shake myself to get my bearings. "What the heck is wrong with you? No decent man grabs a woman and seduces her like that."

His smile is lopsided and unbearably charming. "Who said I was decent?"

My turn to snort. "You're right. My bad."

"Nothing a little bit of your attention can't fix." He grins in that infuriating way that makes me grind my teeth.

His eyes light up as I raise my arms to pull off my fuzzy sweater. Then they dim down when he sees I'm wearing a tee shirt underneath.

He sits on the sofa and crosses his arms. Like he's here to stay. Same as the puppy.

"You think you're so cute, don't you?" I snap, as I fill the kettle with water to make tea.

"No, but you do."

I groan. "I knew you were going to say that."

"Well, then let's discuss serious stuff. Like . . . our new puppy's name."

"I don't know about you but I'm starving." As if to confirm its state, my stomach, which finally feels more settled, growls loudly.

"Plus the puppy will need to eat later." I swing around. "Where will we find dog food at this hour? Is the grocery store still open?"

He leaps up. "I'm on it. You relax and drink your tea." He makes a face at the word *tea*.

In two strides he's at the door unlocking it. "I'll be back. Don't leave."

I shake my head at the implication that he can order me around. What's the use? This man is used to being the leader. The alpha. The one in charge.

He's got a few things to learn about my side of the fence though.

Chapter Twenty-Nine

While I drink a mug of tea curled up on the floor next to the puppy, who is snoring his little head off, I think back to when I first met Salvador on the flight to Athens.

We joked around and talked passionately about the things we love. Football for him. Books for me.

Then he invited me to his football game. He took me to the VIP section and made sure the bartender took care of me.

Afterward, we hung out at a party in Athens on an official date. I felt comfortable around him as he introduced me to his teammates and coaches.

Comfortable enough to kiss him with deep passion at the end of the night.

Then yesterday, we spent hours together with his daughter.

This morning, we drove to the animal shelter together. Then we drove back without our puppy. I shiver at the memory of saying goodbye to the bad boy. That was awful.

And lastly, he proudly showed off his restaurant to me.

The one common denominator in all our encounters is Salvador's supreme self-confidence.

It's got to be what makes him a world-class athlete and icon. A cool dad. And a business owner.

If I hadn't worked on developing my own self-confidence, it would be difficult being around someone like him.

People like Salvador Torres who dominate every space they're in could make a person feel unsure.

I can imagine what would happen to a woman who wasn't as sure of herself as he is.

She'd resent the guy. Being with him would be a challenge. And not an easy one.

Not that I'm considering being *that* companion. No way. He dates supermodels and *"It"* girls. Whatever those are.

The only time I've seen holes in Salvador's confidence was when Danielo his best friend hugged me in Athens.

And when I went into the bathroom today to talk on my phone.

Why does he seem a bit paranoid?

No Google search will ever reveal what truly makes Salvador Torres tick.

I suppose that's true for everyone.

You can read information, but you'll never get to the heart of a person without talking to them, inhaling their essence, touching their skin, and . . . I don't know, tasting their kisses?

I look up guiltily at the tall, gorgeous man entering the apartment. His masculinity permeates the energy in the room. Making anything with life fully aware of his presence.

The puppy whimpers in his sleep as Salvador approaches.

Even the plants seem to coyly tilt their leaves towards him.

He settles a large bag of dog food on a chair and another pretty pink bag with a carry handle on the counter.

Yummy smells come from the pink bag. "I hope you like Indian food," he says. "This place has the best in Portugal. It's my favorite."

"How'd you get it so fast?"

"Woman, I have my ways."

His six-foot-four frame blocks the light from the lamps as he hovers in the threshold between the bedroom and the living room.

"Can you at least sit down so I can see this baby?" I grumble. "You're blocking the light."

"*Our* baby," Salvador chuckles and sits down on the floor right next to me.

"Come here, you," he says, nuzzling my neck and pulling me onto his lap.

"What are you *doing*?" I ask exasperatedly. But I'm not really annoyed. It just sounds good to my ears to be annoyed with him.

"I'm apologizing to you. For being a jerk back at my restaurant."

"Yeah, that was very uncool."

"I know. I have some trust issues I'm working on."

"I'm sorry to hear that."

"Don't be sorry. I'm handling it."

"You need to work on it some more."

"I will. I can do anything I put my mind to. I didn't even know I still had those issues until you came along."

"Oh." I lean backward so my head rests on his chest. I don't want to be so comfortable with him. But I can't help it. He feels so right.

"I'm sorry that I triggered your issues," I murmur.

"Don't be. It means I really like you. That makes me . . . a bit scared."

"Whoa, did you just admit you're scared? Big bad Salvador Torres?"

"Are you making fun of me?"

I shut my mouth. This man is opening up to me and being vulnerable.

"Now I'm being a jerk. I'm sorry."

I can't see his face, but I feel a smile cross his lips as they slide along my neck.

"You do things to me that no one has done in a very long time. I could love you, Corrine Walker."

My body freezes. "You hardly know me."

"I know plenty. And I trust my instincts. My instincts are never wrong."

"Your instincts are never wrong?"

"No scratch that. I was wrong once. But that's not happening to me again."

He leans back, his hands spread behind him on the floor, holding up both our weights.

"How do you know your instincts are right this time?" I ask. He's got to be joking about falling in love with me.

But he doesn't sound like it when he says, "I know that you're gorgeous."

I scoff. "The secret of true love is *not* looks."

"Hush." He kisses my head.

"You're smart. You're a great sister. You love your family. You love kids. And puppies. Well, this puppy anyway. You care about your neighbors. And the city I love."

"Hmmm."

"You enjoyed my football game, and you love to eat good food and drink sangria. What else do I need to know?" He wraps his arms around me and squeezes me tight.

A rush of pure pleasure fills me from head to toe. I must admit I love his full-body hugs as much as I like looking at him. But real relationships require more than that!

"You don't know everything," I say seriously. "I have issues, too."

"I hope one day you can tell me anything. You won't have to hide in a bathroom."

"Maybe," I murmur.

"Definitely," he says with his annoying confidence.

I decide to ignore it. "Thank you for rescuing my puppy."

"*Our* puppy," he growls.

At that moment mister bad boy himself pops up his head and stares at us in a *what are you fools doing on the floor* way.

Arf! He leaps out of the basket and lands on my lap.

Salvador and I laugh together as the puppy wiggles and jumps around us. As happy to see us as we are to see him.

"Stop it!" I squeal as the puppy licks his pink tongue across my cheek.

Salvador groans. "He's giving you more kisses than I am. I'll have to fix that."

In one swift motion, Salvador stands up, plucks me up in his arms, and strides into the kitchen.

"Dinner time."

Arf!

I'm laughing too hard to protest.

Chapter Thirty

"How about Sebastian? He kind of looks like a Sebastian." I stab another delicious mini samosa with my fork and look across at Salvador and Sylvia.

My neighbor joined us for Indian food and puppy-naming after our laughter interrupted her beloved *Bachelor* show.

"No men's names. I'll get jealous." Salvador pours puppy chow out in one of my Tupperware bowls and sits back down.

"Don't be a bobo," Sylvia says, rolling her eyes at Salvador. "You're a star footballer and a business tycoon."

"Right, what she said."

Sylvia had been delighted to meet Salvador Torres and had winked at least three times at me.

I ignored her hints that Salvador was anything good for me.

"Doesn't mean I want to yell 'Sebastian' all over the city's parks," he argues.

"Fine," I grumble. "Let's name him after my favorite dessert. Tiramisu."

Sylvia's turn to shake her head. "Not. Too dangerous. It'll tempt us to eat cake every day."

"Great," I mutter. "No men's names. No food."

I get up and open the bottle of red wine I had saved for a

"

special occasion. I can't think of anything more special than celebrating our new puppy.

I pour out three glasses as I smile to myself. Tonight is indeed very special.

I share my concern that I'd have to leave Porto in one year. "Will I be able to take him home to Maine?"

"Let's cross that bridge when we get to it." Salvador dangles a stuffed toy at the puppy. He bought it enough toys and food to last a year.

"I need to know so I can start scheduling the necessary tests and paperwork."

"Do we have to talk about you and our puppy leaving me right now?" He pulls the toy away making the puppy leap high.

"No," I say. "But you can't ignore the future."

"Who says that'll be the future?" he answers grouchily. "Anyway, let's focus on the immediate concern. We still don't have a name for him."

Between bites of Indian food, sips of red wine, and a lot of barks from our new puppy vying for our attention, we end up discarding name after name until my notepad is filled with scrawled lines.

All possible names are shot down for different reasons. Sylvia vetoes names based on their meanings. And whether they are a good fit for this pup.

Salvador complains some are weak sounding, and some too fancy.

How about, "Goalie?" I ask excitedly thinking he will approve.

"No. It'll be strange for me to walk around saying 'goalie," all the time.

"I just want to name him something cute and fun to match his sparkly personality," I say, weary of the task at hand. "But if you guys can't agree on a name, I'm going to officially call him 'Bad Boy.'"

"No," Sylvia groans. "I promise we'll find the perfect name for him."

We all get quiet. Salvador sits cross-legged on the floor with the puppy now.

Sylvia bites her lips far away in thought.

Me, I sip my wine. And stare at the bridge.

"I got it!"

"What?" Two pairs of human eyes and one pair of canine eyes swing toward me giving their full attention.

"I know you'll both like it."

"Tell us, darling."

Arf!

The puppy's front paws hang across the bottom rungs of my chair. His little face hovers by my leg as he wags his tail to his own personal rhythm.

"It's sparkly, sweet, a tribute to Porto, and your signature brand." I point at Salvador.

He screws up his forehead. "You want us to name him *Salvador*?"

Before I can say anything, he beams. "I don't mind. I like it. We can call him Salvador, Junior."

I groan. "No, you bobo. Here, drink your *wine*." I stress the last word hoping he'll get the hint.

He doesn't. "Thanks," he says in a muffled voice like I hurt his feelings.

Sylvia yelps. "I know!" She raises her hand and waves it.

"You don't have to raise your hand, Sylvia," I say, giggling.

She drops it. Her eyes sparkle with delight. She pokes Salvador's arm. "Don't *you* know?"

"No," he grouses.

I pick up the puppy and scratch behind his ears. He slumps onto my lap. I circle his ears with my fingers enjoying the silky feel of his fur.

"Go ahead, Sylvia."

She turns to Salvador. "Sangria!"

"What?"

"*Sangria*. It's perfect for him. He's got reddish brown fur. And it represents Porto. And your restaurant. Even you can't complain about it."

Salvador looks at the puppy. "Sangria?"

The puppy raises his head. *Arf!*

Laughter rings out in the room.

"Sangria it is, then," Salvador smiles at me. "We've named our first baby."

First baby?

This man is delusional.

Chapter Thirty-One

When you're suddenly hoisted into a world of new people, a new job, a boisterous puppy, and a pig-headed man, a normal calendar and planner don't cut it.

There are three daily walks with Sangria. Not schedulable.

Playtime with Sangria. Non-stop!

Tutoring with Izzy three afternoons each week which Salvador insisted I start right away. That I could schedule.

But then they began asking me to stay for dinner.

Next thing you know, I'm eating dinner and sometimes playing board games with Salvador, Izzy, and his aunt when Salvador is in town. Because they need me to make up two teams.

The whole not dating my boss is working out superbly. Playing board games with the family are *not* dates.

What is great is the income I'm earning to help pay for rent without worrying I'll get an eviction notice.

It helps a lot that I can bring Sangria with me to tutor Izzy. She learns faster when he's around. I shamelessly use him to bargain with her.

She can pet him twice if she gets two words correct. So far, it's working like a charm. Teachers need to think about using puppies as incentives in school.

But there are also my *Writers and Poets* meetings twice a week, which although Carlos broke the ice for me, I'm still not getting any interest or requests for my translation work.

And, let's not forget, my upcoming date with Carlos.

I do not mention the date to Salvador, but I confide in Sylvia about it.

She helps me get ready for it.

"I'm so impressed with your designer eye," I tell her as she pairs a slinky tank top with black jeans from my closet and a wrap-around flowy-sleeved cashmere shawl from her own wardrobe.

"I feel as if I'm borrowing clothes from my mom," I whisper.

Sylvia doesn't know it, but I haven't brought up my mother so often in a long time.

It feels like Mom is here with me, a part of the excitement of Portugal.

Sylvia pats my arm. "In a way you are. I feel as if your mother wants me to share with you. There is a force telling me to watch out for you."

"Really?"

"Really. There are things in this world that humans cannot explain. Things that go far beyond our comprehension."

"Thank you," I say, loading more meaning into the two words than I could express to her.

"Now, tell me who you're dating from your dating site. How is it going with your blast from the past?"

She grins. She's refused to tell me his name until it becomes more of a romance and less of a dating site experience.

"When are you seeing him again?" I ask.

"Tomorrow night. But I have a bike riding date tomorrow afternoon along the sea promenade. With a different man." She has the nerve to blush.

"What! You're dating two guys?"

She shoos me. "Same as you."

"What do you mean? I'm not dating two men."

She gives me a side-eye. "Do not mislead yourself, chickadee. You may be going out with Carlos tonight. But Salvador will be back in town on Monday."

I scoff. "Salvador is my boss. We're not dating."

Sylvia grins and points at Sangria lying flat on his stomach on the floor, his four paws spread out in four different directions.

He had been playing with toy after toy, dragging them out from his toy basket.

Now, they're strewn all over the floor ready to trip me up in my heels.

"Tell Sangria you're not dating his daddy," she chuckles.

I frown. "Yeah, he would not like it one bit."

Sangria is crazy for me, crazy for Izzy, but most of all for Salvador. As soon as he sees Salvador, his tail wags reach a frantic level.

He yelps loudly until he gets Salvador's full attention.

Salvador always gets down on one knee to ruffle his head and stroke his ears.

If his teammates could see how the powerful Salvador Torres turns into a little boy around Sangria, they'd think they'd found his weakness.

But they'd be wrong. Salvador Torres's only weakness, as far as I can tell, is his jealous streak.

And right now, I'm hoping he never finds out I'm going on a date with another man.

I don't owe him my fidelity. But I sure as heck don't want to feel his wrath because he may *believe* I do.

"Sylvia, if a man tells you he loves you and you don't say it back, what does it mean to him?"

Her eyes meet mine in the mirror as she twists my long hair into a French braid. "It depends on the man. If it's a man like my long-ago boyfriend, he will pack up and leave the country."

"Oh," I say numbly.

"But if it's a man like Salvador Torres . . .."

"Let's say it *is* Salvador Torres," I mutter.

"Then, it means, he'll do *whatever it takes* to make sure you fall in love with him, too."

"Great, just what I was afraid of."

Chapter Thirty-Two

hatever it takes.

Sylvia's words ring in my head as I sit across from Carlos at an intimate table for two in the cutest little restaurant near the Dom Luís I Bridge.

It's tucked away in the Ribeira neighborhood, down a side alleyway on cobblestone streets where the pastel-colored houses lean into each other like weary soldiers.

This area of Porto has been around for centuries. It is the colorful, picturesque historic center of the city and is filled with small bars and eateries. It's been named a UNESCO Heritage site.

Before finding the restaurant, Carlos and I walked along the river's promenade toward the bridge.

We searched and found the metal plaque on the wall that we'd heard about in class.

The Portuenses, as the locals were called, lit candles by the plaque to honor the Portuenses who died in the clash with Napolean's troops on the Ponte das Barcas, or bridge of boats.

Thousands of civilians who were fleeing Napolean's army drowned in the Douro River right here.

It felt surreal to be standing in the spot where thousands of people lost their lives.

Carlos and I had gripped hands as if neither of us could bear the weight of that tragedy alone.

Now, sitting in this beautiful enclave of a dining spot, I breathe out and focus on more promising news.

Carlos tells me he's been selected to paint a mural outside a bank that's opening in a month.

"You're an artist?"

He smiles. "It is my passion and my paycheck. I'm a very lucky man. I paint large murals that take forever. I stay employed because they can't get rid of me. But I also paint smaller canvases that I hope I can showcase in a real art gallery one day."

I choke on my wine. "That's incredible, Carlos."

He turns his hands palm up. "It's what I love to do."

"I'd love to see your work. Are there any murals I can check out?"

He frowns. "Check out?"

"Um . . . go to see them."

His smile returns. "Yes, I would be honored. I also have a lot at my home."

The server takes our order and I sit back, relaxing in the simple space, with whitewashed walls, bare cut wooden floors, candles in jars, and flowering plants.

"This place looks like a painting," I remark.

"What would you name this painting?"

I tilt my head, taking in the details all around us. "Promises," I say. "Because . . . um . . . ."

He holds up a hand. "May I?"

I nod, "Yes, tell me."

He leans back in his chair. Intelligent brown eyes sweep the room with one glance. "It is bare enough for you to see your own vision, to paint your own plans. And pretty enough to inspire you."

"Wow, you nailed it."

"I hammered the point?"

I laugh. "No, nailed it means you got it perfectly."

"Okay, then I'm happy I nailed it."

The rest of our dinner date is like an interview with Carlos asking me about my life back in Maine with my sisters.

Then I ask him about his home in Brazil.

I love learning about his culture, but it feels more like a class project than a Friday night date.

I can't put a finger on what's wrong, or different, or not working.

But maybe that's how all first dates are supposed to go. It's a getting-to-know-you process.

Except Salvador and I never have any of these awkward silences. I never feel as if I must think up something to say when I'm with him.

Stop it, Corrine, I scold myself. Stop comparing. Of course, Carlos is not Salvador, with Salvador's cocky macho ways.

I should be grateful to have a sweet, wonderful artist interested in me instead.

As we walk back down the promenade, we stop to listen to musicians and enjoy a magic show, all played in the crisp air.

October is by far the most perfect month in Porto. Fewer tourists and more locals buzzing about give the city a different energy. I feel as if I'm a local, too.

"Do you have a boyfriend?" Carlos asks suddenly, as we stand side by side watching a young man play a guitar and sing a love song in Portuguese.

Salvador Torres's face pops into my head. I push it out. Or try to, but his sexy smile, bear hugs, and steamy kisses bring a smile to my face.

Am I going to deny his existence? Of course, I am. Because he is *not* my boyfriend. Despite what Sylvia believes.

Carlos steps forward and drops a few euros in the guitarist's basket.

"No." The word comes out in a chokehold. "I do not," I say firmly. "I do not."

I'm talking like a drunk person trying to sound sober.

Carlos doesn't look at me. He's staring across to the other side of the river. "Too bad."

"What?"

"In Brazil, we say, 'Never poke a jaguar with a short stick.'"

I ponder his words for a moment. "Is that like how we say, 'don't poke the bear?'"

"Probably," he says glumly.

"Who's the jaguar in our scenario?" I laugh, trying to make light of the conversation.

Carlos turns serious eyes on me. "The man you cannot name."

Chapter Thirty-Three

When I step off the elevator and turn to follow Carlos down his hallway, my heart pounds.

I should have listened to my gut. I should not have agreed to come home with him.

Now, I'm going to have to deal with this awkward situation.

As Carlos walks beside me, my heart lurches.

I don't want him to get the wrong idea. I didn't lead him on.

I didn't flirt. I didn't kiss him. I didn't say, "Take me home with you."

None of that.

And yet, here I am.

But how could I have refused his invitation to see his artwork in progress? I couldn't. He was too sweet and genuine and passionate.

And I'd felt bad for hemming and hawing about whether I had a boyfriend.

Carlos had glossed over the topic of *the man I cannot name* and continued talking about art.

He'd explained that before he started on murals, he created the entire image on canvas. He wanted to show me some of his works in progress.

To get my opinion.

I must admit, I feel flattered he wants my opinion.

I did come to Porto to meet artists and writers and here's the perfect opportunity to be a part of that world.

I just don't know why my stomach is all in knots as we enter his dark apartment.

Like I'm being unfaithful to Salvador. Which I'm not.

"Carlos, I'm not sure . . .," I stutter.

But then he flips on the light switch. The world changes from darkness to a kaleidoscope of colors and images.

It's like walking into a fairyland and ripping off your blindfold.

"Oh, my goodness!" I cover my mouth. I can't speak. I can only stare at the walls.

There are paintings stacked up against the walls. Canvases are hung on the walls and leaning against them.

There are large pieces, medium-sized pieces, small pieces.

The overpowering scents of oil paint and turpentine invade my senses as an integral part of this new world.

The studio apartment is barely large enough for Carlos and all his paintings.

"These are incredible!"

"Thank you."

Carlos stands beside me, his dark eyes staring at me intently.

Not in the way that Salvador looks at me, with playful adoration, but with a deep mystical aura. As if intuiting my reaction to his deep passion project.

I walk around the tiny room inspecting the images closer.

I see the details of towering trees, and hidden animals amidst the rainforest, their stripes or spots appearing and disappearing.

There are gray smoky clouds and raging fires. Beautiful dark-skinned angels.

"I feel as if I can see right into your soul," I whisper.

"My home inspires me," Carlos says simply.

I nod silently. I see so much of a country and a man's love and fears in the images.

This is more revealing than all the answers he gave to my questions at dinner.

Wouldn't it be great if instead of answering questions to describe ourselves to strangers, we could walk around with our passion in our arms and show them instead?

They'd know about us immediately, no questions needed.

I want to do this here with my own work. I want to translate an author's vision. The way Carlos has translated his own here.

"Your art inspires me. It makes me want to do something meaningful and important with my own talents."

A huge grin lights up his face. "That is the best response I've ever had to my art. Thank you."

"I can't wait to see the murals in person."

"You are very kind, Corrine."

I shake my head. "No, I mean it."

I look up at Carlos. He's smiling at me. My heart fills with a feeling I can't describe.

I'll have to ask Sylvia. It's not the same feeling that I have when I'm with Salvador.

But that's a good thing, right?

Maybe this is what you're supposed to feel in a real relationship. Mutual respect and admiration.

Not like you want to throw yourself at a man and kiss his lips forever. I have to ask someone.

Maybe I'll ask Ava and Bridget. They've found their true loves.

"You have made my day," Carlos says interrupting my thoughts. "Would you like some wine?"

"Yes, please."

I follow Carlos into his kitchen area. He pours us both a glass of red wine.

I sip mine slowly, still admiring the paintings.

"Is that the one you're working on now?"

I point to a canvas leaning against the wall.

"Yes."

"May I see it?"

"Of course."

Carlos sets his wine glass down and lifts the canvas off the floor. He brings it over to where I'm standing.

I stare at the painting.

It's a beautiful landscape. A lake with mountains in the background. A tree line on one side.

The colors are vibrant and alive.

"This is beautiful," I say. "Is this a real place?"

"Yes."

"It looks like a place I would love to visit." I look at Carlos. "Where is it?"

"It's in the Azores islands. It's called Lagoa Azul. Blue Lake. You would love it. You should go some time. I'll take you."

"That would be nice." I don't know what else to say.

We stand there awkwardly.

I thought being with an artist would be easy. We'd have lots to talk about. The conversation would flow.

We'd laugh and joke around like it was when we were with a crowd.

But alone together, it's a bit . . . I hate to say this . . . awkward. Like we're both trying hard.

What's wrong with me?

As if sensing my disconnect, Carlos touches me lightly on my hand.

"I had a good time tonight, Corrine." He sounds formal and polite.

"So did I."

"You are a beautiful woman. I'm lucky you went out with me."

"No, I'm the lucky one. Your paintings are amazing."

"You have no idea how much that means to me."

Carlos leans forward and kisses me on the cheek.

My phone vibrates in my purse.

I take it out. It's a text from Salvador.

"Where are you?"

I feel an instant bristling at his abrupt manner and a simultaneous rush of excitement to talk to him.

Something is definitely wrong with me.

Why can't I break this addiction I seem to have to men who are completely the opposite of what I want? Why can't I connect with good guys like Carlos on a deeper level?

This is so frustrating.

I tell Carlos I have to leave, and he walks me downstairs. He waits with me while I call a ride-share.

"Thanks again," I say. "It was truly eye-opening. I mean that."

"Yes, but I didn't nail it."

"What?" My eyebrows shoot up.

"I didn't get it perfectly." His dark eyes gleam under the streetlight. I can read disappointment clearly in them.

"Maybe don't use that expression too much," I suggest lightly. "But for the record, your art is on point."

He shakes his head. "What's up with you Americans and your nails and points?"

I laugh as my ride appears. "See you soon, Carlos."

As I settle back into the car seat, I text Salvador.

"I'm on my way home."

"What time will you be there?"

"Soon."

"Good, I can't go to sleep until I talk to you. And tomorrow is the big game."

My stomach does a flip.

Salvador is in Croatia, in a different time zone, and over a thousand miles from me.

But somehow, I feel closer to him than I do to Carlos who is mere feet away.

Chapter Thirty-Four

After returning to my apartment and chatting by text with Salvador for a few minutes I go to Sylvia's.

She's pet-sitting Sangria for me, so first I snuggle with him. I can't help the baby talk that escapes my lips whenever I see his little face.

He yaps at me. I spin him around the room. "Seriously, who needs men when I have you?"

"Maybe you should sit down and tell me about your date." Sylvia points me to a chair in her kitchen and starts making coffee.

"I had a nice time," I say, taking off her pretty shawl and draping it on a hangar. "But I felt conflicted."

"Ah," she said knowingly. "Carlos isn't Salvador."

"No one is Salvador," I admit. "That doesn't mean he's right for me."

"Maybe. Maybe not." Sylvia settles into her seat after handing me a cup of strong dark coffee. I'll be up all night after this caffeine.

"Carlos is a student, an artist, and a sweet guy. And Salvador is an older man, with a baby, a bar, and a career that puts him in the limelight, surrounded by supermodels." I end with, "Is there even a choice here? I should be with Carlos, right?"

"Not necessarily," she says. "Both are great choices. You should choose the one who captures your heart."

I shake my head. "No, it should be the one who matches with me. That whole '*the heart wants what the heart wants*' philosophy always ends badly for me."

Sylvia frowns, her forehead bunched up like an accordion.

"Maybe you need to understand who *you* are before you can choose who you want to be with."

"That was what I told my sister Bridget a few months ago and now she's happily engaged."

Sylvia beams. "See, the advisor needs to take her own advice."

I snort. "And they say I'm the smart sister."

Sylvia pats my hand. "You are perfect."

"Not perfect enough."

"Perhaps you should consult your sisters. You've told me a lot about them. They sound like the people who know you best. They can help you figure out what's holding you back."

"Holding me back from what?"

Sylvia collects our cups and heads toward the kitchen.

Sangria springs from my lap to follow her in case any tidbits of food may be forthcoming.

I wait patiently for her to return. When she does, she hands me a notebook.

"What is this?"

"This will be your journal. I want you to write in it every morning when you wake up. After you walk Sangria, take some time, just fifteen minutes for yourself, and write about you."

"Why do I need to do that? I have planners to keep track of all my activities."

She pats the cover of the simple black and white notebook. "Because here is where you'll discover the answers to your innermost questions."

I eye the innocent book with skepticism. "This can tell me which man to choose. Like creating a pros and cons list?"

I flip the pages, fanning them, eyeing their emptiness, hoping to find some answers.

Sylvia laughs merrily. "It's not magic. You must work at it."

I groan. "I have enough work right now."

"But not one thing you're doing now is as important as this." She says it so firmly I feel she knows what she's talking about.

"Okay, I will write in the journal every morning for a week. To see if it can help me make a good decision."

"And call your sisters," she adds.

"Yes, I'll do that, too."

I leave with Sangria and take him outside for a quick walk around the garden.

"Why is life so complicated?" I ask him.

He plonks down on his haunches and stares at me as if to say, "Don't ask me."

Chapter Thirty-Five

Getting my sisters together on a conference video call is a great idea in *theory*.

We're scattered in different cities, countries, and time zones. It's extremely difficult to arrange, but we managed to do it.

Bridget is seated at her laptop on the Greek island of Aegina in front of the gorgeous olive grove belonging to her fiancé's family.

Her love story is unique. She fell in love with her best friend. Someone she went from talking to every single day for months to realizing he is her one true love. I don't think she can shed any light on my situation.

And Ava, my oldest sister, fell in love with her old high school crush.

Ava stands, holding her phone in her brand new business, *Hazel's Gelato*, named after our mother.

Daisy, a freshman in college, is in her dorm room, sitting cross-legged on her bed, munching Doritos and playing with Freckles, her cat. She's fortunate to get into a pet-friendly college with an actual Pet Wing in its dorms.

Then there's Emerald, or Emmie, as we call our baby sister who is a senior in high school.

When I see all their faces on my screen, tears prick my eyes. I am not the crying sister, so I quickly swipe them away off-screen.

I don't want them worrying about me.

The first thing we talk about is Dad. Ava, who's back living at home to oversee Emerald's last year of high school, announces that Dad and Maxine seem to be drifting apart.

"That's tough," I say. "How's Dad doing?"

Ava looks up at the ceiling, one hand on her chin then back at us, her eyes serious. "I think he's lonely. But I'm glad he's dating."

"Too bad I can't introduce him to Sylvia," I tell my sisters about my beautiful neighbor. "Dad deserves love and happiness just like everyone else. And me too."

My sisters stare at me in total silence like I'm a stranger.

"What?" I ask.

"You feeling alright, sis?" Ava asks. "You've never talked like this."

"Yeah, how're the hot footballers you showed up with in Athens a few months ago?" Bridget teases.

I take my time thinking about how to answer.

At that moment Sangria wakes up from napping in a spot of sunshine on the floor and dashes across the room to my chair.

He balances on his hind legs, his front paws on my legs. He barks excitedly at the screen. My sisters squeal back at him.

"He's so cute."

"Hi, Sangria."

I pick up Sangria from the floor and present his wiggly body for my sisters' viewing.

"Look Freckles, you have a cousin," Daisy waves one of her cat's paws at the screen.

Sangria barks. Arf! Arf!

Everyone laughs and I feel like I'm back at home hanging out in the kitchen, making muffins and talking about school and boys.

If I want their opinion on how I should handle the Carlos versus Salvador situation, I need to speak up before they digress onto other topics.

I know my sisters. It's like we have collective ADHD. We distract each other endlessly.

I put two fingers in my mouth and whistle loudly.

Everyone stops talking over each other and stares at me. Even Sangria has stopped yapping and is looking at me.

He's heard my whistle many times. But usually, it's to stop him from doing something mischievous. He tilts his head in a "Who me?" look.

"It's okay, boy, you didn't do anything wrong." I scratch his head.

"Wow, Corrine, living abroad has changed you a lot."

I take a deep breath. "I guess." If they only knew.

I plunge in. "I'm caught between two men, and I don't know who to choose."

Total silence descends again.

Then chaos erupts as they all start talking at once. I almost whistle again but I don't want to upset Sangria.

When they finally settle down, I launch into the dilemma.

"As you guys know, my partner picker is off. I choose the wrong guy every time."

My sisters screw up their faces in four versions of confusion.

"What are you talking about Corrine?" Ava asks. "You date the hottest guys. The ones who ride motorcycles, wear leather jackets, and look like Michael B. Jordan."

"Yeah, I have always had a secret crush on your boyfriends. Every single one of them," Daisy admits. "Not that they'd ever consider dating a goody-two-shoes like me."

Bridget holds up a hand. "Is this about you wanting to change your hipster smart girl loves bad boy image?"

I scoff. "I'm not a hipster!"

Emerald seems entranced by the discussion. I've heard from Bridget that Emmie's dating a boy who is comfortable breaking the rules. I hope she doesn't follow in my footsteps.

As I listen to my sisters rave about the guys I've dated and their perception of me as the cool, brainy sister with all the luck dating hot guys, I realize there's so much they don't know about me.

So much they have wrong. Like everything they know is fake news. But whose fault is that?

"Maybe we should start at the beginning," I tell them. "How much time do you all have?"

Every single sister says she's there for the whole enchilada.

And I begin.

It helps that they're all grown women now. Even Emerald.

Finally, I feel like I can share the stuff I've kept inside for years. It helps that I've been writing in Sylvia's journal every day for the past week up until this call.

"Did you guys know I had an eating disorder starting when I was twelve years old?"

The gasps that emanate from the screen tell me they had no idea.

"Tell us everything, Corrine. Please," says Ava.

I sigh heavily. "Can I just read it to you instead?" I open the journal.

Sylvia was right. Once I started journaling every morning, I found it easy to dive deep into topics I hadn't ever discussed with anyone but my therapist.

I read some entries, touching on my journey from age eleven when our mom passed away. To now.

Exactly ten years.

Whenever I glance up from reading, I come face to face with expressions of shock and pity on their faces.

Before I'm halfway through relaying my struggles with my eating disorder, my years in therapy, my choosing unavailable boys to date and them breaking my heart each time, my sisters are in tears and sobbing openly.

I stop talking. "It's not my intention to make you guys feel sad or guilty or anything like that."

They hush me and insist I keep reading from my journal.

Sangria sits quietly on my lap as I read. As if he senses I need his comfort to get through this.

I stroke his fur as I turn the pages, not censoring my words, thoughts, or feelings for the first time ever.

When I close the book, my sisters all stand up and clap, following Ava's lead as she's already standing up.

I feel my face heating up. "I'm sorry I couldn't share any of this with you guys before now. I was so ashamed. I'm ashamed now."

Bridget speaks first. "You better not be embarrassed you shared that with us. I don't know about Ava, but I'm so sorry I didn't notice you were suffering all by yourself."

Ava can't seem to form words. She waves her hand in front of her face as if to say, 'not now.' The copious amount of tears streaming down her face tells me everything though.

I kept my distress over Mom's death a secret from them because I thought I had to be strong and brave, but it was misguided. I was wrong. I can see that now.

Daisy wipes away her tears and says, "It's always okay to say you're not okay."

My sisters nod as one.

"Especially to us. You must know you can say anything to us," Ava recovers and says with great force. "Otherwise, what is the point of having sisters?"

I smile at the girls, now women, who have strived to find their own paths and live with their own grief every day. "I want you guys to know, I admire you all."

"Thank you," Emerald is the first to say. "We love you, Corrine. I must admit I've wanted to be like you. Dating hot athletes and not giving a hoot if the relationship ended. You'd just go on your merry way."

I stifle a laugh. "Fake news, girlfriend. I was always devastated."

"But you never told us. Or showed us," Bridget frowns.

"You were all dealing with your own stuff. But if you're interested now, I do have a dilemma trying to decide who I should date."

"Give us the tea," Daisy laughs.

As I tell my sisters about Salvador and Carlos, I feel a sense of relief.

Like I've stepped aside and let go of the proverbial Sisyphus rock I'd been pushing up the mountain every day for the past ten years.

I welcome their advice. Their criticisms, their questions. I embrace all the feedback that comes with having four very different personalities weigh in on my romantic life.

It's my youngest sister, Emerald who asks the most insightful question.

"Who is it that you think about when you first wake up and

right before you go to sleep at night? That is the one you should pick."

"Salvador Torres," I say. "Without a doubt."

"Well?" Emmie says. "That's the one."

"But what if I'm only gravitating toward him because he's the type I always go for?"

"Is he the type you always go for?" asks Daisy. "It doesn't sound like it. If a man gives you a puppy, he's a keeper to me."

Sangria barks in agreement.

"Don't go for the safe choice, sis," Ava, the most safety-conscious person I know advises. "You could miss out on something extraordinary."

"Go hot, or go home," says Bridget, our lovely sister who is lucky her man has killer abs. "A little challenge is not a bad thing. Just be sure you're true to yourself."

"Maybe reinventing myself is too calculated."

"Yes," they exclaim as one.

"Maybe . . ." I stop and ponder. They wait patiently, watching me from their corners of the world.

"Maybe I should focus on . . ." I scrunch up my forehead. I can feel the answer inside me wanting to come out.

Words flash through my mind. Focus on discovering myself, focus on what I want. Focus on what makes sense. But I don't say any of those things.

"You know what it is," Ava encourages.

"Focus on how I feel. Not only when I'm with Salvador. But when I'm by myself."

My sisters cheer.

"I think focusing on how you feel is a great idea," Daisy says. "Your gut is usually on target."

"And write it in your journal," Ava says. "We want to hear about it next week."

Sangria and I say goodbye to my sisters.

Ava stays on the phone after everyone hangs up. She asks if I need to get a therapist in Porto. And how I'm handling being away from mine.

"Tell me how I can help you," she says. "I am devastated I didn't know that you needed me."

"I didn't need you, Ava," I cry. "I needed Mom."

Chapter Thirty-Six

I tap my pen on the edge of my journal and stare out the window at the Dom Luís I Bridge. A steaming cup of tea sits next to me.

It's the first week of November. I've just come back in from walking Sangria.

I had to brush his coat to dislodge the twigs and leaves caught in his fur after he'd rolled on his back in the grass.

The trees have shed their multi-colored leaves, pieces of which now litter my apartment.

"Bad boy," I pretended to admonish Sangria.

Arf! He licked my face and raced around in circles.

Now he's sitting by my feet as I do my daily fifteen minutes of journal writing.

Midterms are approaching and students are spending more time in the library and less in cafes drinking sangria and flirting with the idea of living permanently as an expat abroad.

I'm still finding it difficult to make inroads with the *Writers & Poets Club*. It's as if they don't take me seriously.

My pen beats harder against the page as I recall the meeting yesterday.

Several male writers asked if my background as a Black woman would affect how I translated their books.

"What do you mean?" I'd asked.

"Well," said one of the writers, "Do you harbor any innate anger or resentment toward us?"

"Toward you?" I still wasn't getting his point. I was stumped on how to respond.

It was Carlos who spoke up and said one word. "Slavery."

I'm aware of the atrocities committed against Africans by the Portuguese for over four hundred years. I'm ever more aware that much of the beautiful city of Porto was financed by the slave trade. But I'd never connected that history to my goal of being a translator of Portuguese books.

My college education and the ability to travel gives me a unique privilege.

One that I'm starting to recognize can open doors for others like me who may want to consider learning languages as a career goal.

I looked at the trio of male writers. Without getting huffy, I said, "My education and experiences highly qualify me to be a translator. Not my skin color. In fact, my heritage is an asset, not a liability."

I smiled diplomatically at them. They didn't return the smile.

Carlos spoke up behind me. "It'll depend on what you write."

They frowned. I knew then I'd never be asked to translate their stories and poems.

It was disheartening to come up against these unexpected barriers. Especially since I've been welcomed by everyone I've met here.

Maybe Salvador has a point. Maybe they're pseudo-intellectuals. They're not open-minded. And often talk as if they are right and everyone else is missing the point.

I'd hung around a bit, hoping someone would approach me and say they were sorry they'd asked me such an insulting question. But no one did.

Later as we'd walked out of the cafe, Carlos had comforted me by saying, "They're not the only writers in Portugal, Corrine. They're just a small handful."

"You're right," I'd said. "I need to expand my world a bit."

But it still hurt a lot. To be rejected before I'd even gotten a chance to show my skills.

I press my pen to the crisp journal paper and begin writing.

Chapter Thirty-Seven

Salvador Torres is sitting next to me in his red sports coupe. The top is down, the breeze is whipping my hair behind me and Sangria, who whined until I pulled him from his basket, is fast asleep on my lap.

Porto is far behind.

We're zooming along the Douro River valley road toward the wine region.

I've gasped more than a few times at the magnificent scenery.

Terraced hillsides showcase neat lines of flaming red-leafed grape trees.

The hillsides are radiant with color and life, the leaves fluttering in the afternoon breeze.

This world we live in is so large. So incredibly beautiful. So welcoming in many ways we don't realize until we step outside our familiar boxes and embrace it all.

My world is expanding right now and so is my ability to understand the new language I'm learning, not a language with words, but one with emotions.

Paying attention to how I feel.

Not being afraid to feel.

As much as I love words, I am beginning to think it's emotions that connect us.

Like this emotion that overtakes my heart as I glance at the man beside me.

His rugged jaw, his crooked smile when he looks over at me, his gray eyes deep with concentration as he steers the vehicle perfectly around the winding road following this ancient river.

I simply have no words, just emotions.

This is joy, plain and simple.

I smile out the window as I stroke Sangria behind his ears.

Every so often, Salvador rests one of his large hands on top of mine, as if making sure I know he's there.

Physical touch must be his love language. I'm not sure what mine is.

Maybe it's the same because I don't mind him caressing me every chance he gets.

As if he's reading my mind, Salvador says suddenly, "You know I love you, right?"

He squints as we turn a corner and the sun shines into his eyes.

I point to the sunglasses perched on top of his head. "Why don't you put on your sunglasses?" I say, ignoring his comment about loving me.

"Because I'd rather see you in the light."

His intensity stuns me. His words are not ironic.

I don't need this right now. I want the joyful bliss I had a few minutes ago.

"You're such a flirt," I tease, aiming for casual and carefree. "I don't believe a word you say."

"Why is it so hard to accept that you're loved."

"Because you're my boss." I don't add, "And the epitome of a bad boy."

His hand is a warm blanket closing around my chilled hands.

He chuckles. "I'm your everything."

I shrug off his hand. "Are you always this arrogant? Or do you practice?"

"Every day," he says with the smile that sells clothes and cologne on billboards around Europe.

I frown. "Are we going to have a fight on this beautiful day?"

His eyebrows arch up. "We can. You won't win. What's your trump card? That I don't know what I feel? Baby, just accept it. Maybe say, thanks."

I stare out the window. Why can't I accept it? I'm focusing on feelings. And I feel great with him. But why is it so hard to believe he loves me? Because too many other guys didn't?

"Thanks," I mumble.

"You are the most beautiful woman I've ever seen. I knew it the moment you offered to take the middle seat on the plane and move the other woman into the window so I could have the aisle seat."

"You are six foot four inches tall. It was the practical thing to do."

He shakes his head. "Most people wouldn't bother. You didn't know me and you were concerned for my comfort. That's the type of person I want in my life. Need in my life."

"Well, you didn't take the aisle. You took the middle seat."

A huge smile lights up his face. "That's because I was afraid with your musical chairs arrangement you'd end up in the window and I'd end up in the aisle and I wouldn't get to sit next to you. I wasn't taking that chance. If I took the middle seat, it would be a win."

I burst out laughing. I don't know how he does it.

Somehow, he always says the right thing. His straightforward honesty is sprinkled with sweetness. It overshadows his arrogance in a heartbeat.

At my laughter, Sangria's head pops up.

Arf!

"Look at how adorable he is," I tell Salvador. Sangria's ears fly out behind him in the breeze. It's getting chilly out, but Sangria is keeping my legs toasty warm.

I look from Salvador to Sangria. "You guys are both weirdos."

"And we both love you."

Arf! Sangria licks my ear. I giggle and push him back down.

"Arf!" Salvador barks and tweaks my ear before putting both hands back on the steering wheel as we descend into the beautiful valley of stone houses, narrow bridges, and sparkling river water.

"Can this day get any better?" I sigh.

"I sure hope so. You haven't kissed me yet."

Chapter Thirty-Eight

Salvador pulls over to a lookout point for me to take photos.

He's got Sangria wrapped up in his arms and they look so cute together that I make Salvador pose with him next to the river.

A few American travelers circle the overlook taking photos from every angle. Their New England accent reminds me of home. None of them recognize Salvador.

One of the women asks if we'd like our picture taken.

Salvador quickly gives her his phone and opens the camera for her. Then he pulls me next to him and beams.

The woman says, "Smile."

He tugs my hand, "Smile, princess."

It's useless trying to fight this man. I lean into him, place a hand on his chest, and tilt my face toward the camera.

His arm feels like it'll never let me go. I let myself sink into the role of being his girlfriend and smile as if we're really a couple.

"Wow, you guys are gorgeous," the woman says handing back Salvador's phone.

I glance at the photo. With the river and vineyards behind us and Sangria looking extra spiffy with a red bow around his neck, we do look like we could be in an ad for a lifestyle magazine.

Salvador thanks the woman and gives her advice on places she and her family may want to see further up the valley.

I walk Sangria to some bushes on the side to do his business.

When we're back in the car, I ask Salvador if we can put up the top.

He climbs out of the car and comes over to my side. I watch confused.

He raises his beefy arms above his head and peels his sweater upward exposing his tight bronzed muscled abdomen.

I almost swoon right then and there.

Get a grip, Corrine. You're not that shallow.

Not like my sister Bridget who was always swooning over Ajax's abs long before she fell in love with him.

"Here, baby. Take this."

He slips the wooly cashmere sweater that smells of his wonderful scent of oranges, musk and baby powder over my head.

I feel as if I'm wearing one of his hugs.

"Thank you." I lean over and kiss his cheek when he climbs back into the car.

He presses a button, and the top of the car slides over us.

As soon as we're in total privacy (except for Sangria), he gathers my face in his hands and stares into my eyes.

"I never want you to feel cold. Or hungry. Or alone. Or scared. Or anything that I can fix for you. Do you hear me, Corrine? All you have to do is tell me. And if anyone ever hurts you, I will kill them." He speaks matter of fact like it's unquestionable.

My head reels at his last words.

Surely, he doesn't mean it. But a look into his fierce gray eyes begs to differ.

This man is not like the boys I dated back home.

He's nothing like the ones who promised to be there for me and then ghosted me when I was sad or depressed.

I don't know for sure if Salvador could handle sadness or depression or any mental illness I've been through trying to stay strong for my family. Trying to be the independent one. The one they didn't have to worry about.

But I have a feeling he's all in. Like he can handle it and if he can't, he'd figure out a way to.

As if sensing I've realized something important about him, he takes that moment to seal our fates with a deep kiss.

I let myself get swept away. I sink into a new world where our two breaths become one.

Chapter Thirty-Nine

"This road here is the most scenic in all of Portugal."

"What's the name of it?" I ask although every road looks stunning to me.

"The N222," Salvador announces.

I hold up my phone to videotape the passing vista.

"Tell me again where we're going?" I ask.

It's been twenty minutes since the monumental kiss at the overlook.

I will never forget the way Salvador's lips felt swooping down on mine, inhaling my very core with his skillful tongue.

"You'll see," he says with a wink.

"Wow!" I exclaim for the hundredth time as a traditional boat sails past.

"I'm running out of battery on my phone," I say, noticing the diminishing charge as I hold it up to take a photo.

Salvador hands me his phone. "Use mine." He rattles off the code to get in.

I hesitate. "You're not supposed to give people the code for your phone."

"Please," he scoffs. "You're not people. Did I miss something, or didn't we just have the kiss of a lifetime?"

I giggle. "You're so dramatic."

Although he's right. It was amazing.

"So, where're we going?" I ask again, punching in the code for his phone so I can capture more of this fairy tale countryside.

"Oh my God," I rush out. I'm staring at Salvador's screen. It's the photo of us and Sangria looking like a family that the passing tourist just snapped.

I can't believe he's made it his screen saver already.

Salvador glances over. "The only one missing to make it a family portrait is Izzy," he says.

"You are delusional, you know. How many times do I have to tell you, we are not an item."

"The same number of times I've told you we are . . . or will be, so don't fight it."

"Stubborn much?" I shake my head.

"In denial much?" He teases.

The truth is, no one compares to Salvador Torres.

Absolutely no one.

Chapter Forty

"Daddy!" Izzy races down the tree-lined driveway and straight into her father's arms.

He gathers her up and spins her around, her little legs flying out behind her.

Sangria leaps out of the car and yaps his little head off.

He plows toward Salvador and Izzy, trotting in circles around Salvador's feet.

Izzy squeals to her father in English, "Let me down."

He gently places her feet on the ground. Immediately, Izzy wraps her arms around the puppy while Sangria licks her face and wiggles his furry body with delight. His white-tipped tail whips back and forth.

Salvador's gray eyes gleam with love as he looks down on his daughter.

He raises his eyes and catches me staring at him. I can't even pretend I was looking around the woodsy driveway because my eyes are glued onto his face.

He winks.

Heat flushes my cheeks.

I shiver and wrap my arms close pulling Salvador's sweater tighter around my body.

He must think I'm anemic the way I'm always shivering in his presence.

"Let's go inside," he says, scooping up Izzy and Sangria in one arm. He leans over and pulls me toward him.

His warm comforting hand surrounds my chilled fingers.

"Baby, your hand is ice cold." He raises it to his lips and kisses my knuckles. His gaze slides down to my lips.

I shake my head no.

He sighs.

My lips rise at the corners. Why is he so cute? And his daughter? She's even cuter than he is.

"Where are we?"

"Come on. I want you to meet my family. That's the surprise."

"Your family? Is this gorgeous countryside area where you grew up?"

He chuckles, "You really should have Googled me, you know."

I swat his arm with my free hand.

Salvador plants a kiss on my forehead.

Izzy covers Sangria's eyes with her chubby hands. "Don't look, Sangria. They are kissing."

Salvador laughs and plants a huge smack on Izzy's forehead accompanied by a long kissy noise.

This time she covers *her* face with her hands.

I don't know if it's Salvador's intention, but it's clear that when we enter his parents' home we already look like a little family.

I've met Salvador's aunt many times at his mansion in Porto. But now I am being presented to his mother and father.

Butterflies tickle my stomach. I glance down at my clothing. It's obvious that I'm wearing their son's sweater, like a love-struck teenager with a crush on the football star.

I groan. "You could have warned me," I whisper out the side of my mouth.

He's too busy laughing and hugging his mother with Izzy still in his arms to respond. But he gives me a reassuring smile.

And honestly, I don't have time to be nervous. Or to straighten my clothing and my flyaway strands of hair.

His father gives my hand a hearty shake and his mom squeezes me tightly in a hug. "Welcome to our home. Salvador has talked a lot about you."

I raise an eyebrow at him. "You have?" I mouth over his mother's head.

He grins.

"I told them everything," he says.

Mrs. Torres pats my arm. "Come and sit down." She guides me to a simple but cozy living room with overstuffed sofas, large ottomans, and floor to ceiling bookcases.

"Wow, can I take a look?"

His mom gestures, "Of course."

"Do you want to see the pool?" Izzy drags me toward sliding glass doors that look out at the Douro River, as well as the surrounding mountains, vineyards, and olive orchards.

The swimming pool is back lit with blue lights reflecting the dusky sky above. It's a magical scene, yet as comfortable as a warm blanket.

Have I walked through a portal into a new world?

"This whole place is stunning," I say.

Mrs. Torres beams at me. "It's too cold to swim now but you

must return in the summer. It's lovely to soak up the Portugal sun while you sip our family's port wine."

"You make your own port wine?" I blurt out.

"We only sell it locally," Mr. Torres explains. "But it's good."

"I bet."

"This is the most beautiful Quinta I've ever seen."

I haven't seen many other farmhouses in Portugal, but can they all be this gorgeous?

As if reading my mind, Mrs. Torres says, "We have a 9.9 rating on the hotel booking websites. For our five cottages scattered around the property." She points me to the sign with the award of 9.9.

"Very impressive indeed."

"Many of the farms have set up guest spaces for visitors to experience living on a real-life Quinta and eating farm-to-table food on the spot." Salvador points to rows of t-shirts and baseball caps lined up in a glass case by the door. "We even have our own merch," he says with a smile.

"How entrepreneurial of you," I laugh.

Mr. Torres hands me a tiny, but elaborately decorated glass filled with red liquid. I sip it slowly. It is easily the best wine I've ever tasted.

"This is from your vineyard?" I ask.

Salvador strides over to the sliding doors. "Over there, that mountainside . . .," he points. "Those are our trees and vines. This port you're drinking is called . . .."

Before he can finish, Izzy chimes in with, "Isabel Grand."

"Right," Salvador says.

"Named after our precious granddaughter," Mr. Torres smiles proudly.

Izzy giggles. "Can we name one after Corrine?"

Salvador grins at me. I make a face at him.

"That is a fantastic idea, baby girl."

Sangria barks in agreement.

I can't even imagine having a wine named after me, so I don't enter into the playful exchange of ideas of what they'd call it.

I gulp in the pure clean mountain air.

"I could stay here forever," I whisper to myself. Or at least I thought it was to myself.

I didn't hear Salvador approaching until I feel his arms around me. "That's the best thing I've heard all year, sweetheart."

I don't fight it. I lean back against his chest and let him hold me close. His soft kisses feel like tiny raindrops on the back of my neck.

"Dinner's ready," Mrs. Torres announces.

Mr. Torres asks what everyone's drinking.

Izzy and Sangria race each other around the room.

A sense of peace descends over me. I didn't know life could be like this with a man.

"Are you okay?" Salvador whispers in my ear.

I nod, blinking back tears.

I can't cry here. His family will think I'm unhinged. Or a drama queen. I bite my lips so I don't shed a tear.

As if he knows, Salvador swings me around and buries my face in his chest. He rubs circles on my back as he murmurs, "I got you, baby. I got you."

A strangled sob escapes my lips. "I know."

And I do know.

Salvador Torres won't let anything happen to me. Ever. Maybe he is the man I need to be with. Maybe it's him after all.

Chapter Forty-One

"Have you guys always lived here?" I ask Salvador as he gives me a tour of the property the next morning, guiding me past olive trees and rosemary plants that are as tall as me.

The air is perfumed with fresh herbs.

"I was born here, but the cottages and the restaurant are new. My parents felt lonely after I left to play football, and my crew stopped hanging out here. They wanted to keep having people around."

"Empty nest syndrome," I murmur. "Something my dad is beginning to experience with Bridget in Greece, me in Portugal, and Daisy in college."

Salvador runs a hand through his hair. "I can't imagine what I'll do when it's my turn to say goodbye to Izzy."

"I doubt you'll be alone," I aim for playful, but it comes out snarky.

It's the first time I've considered that Salvador will probably marry a beautiful woman, have more kids, and live a fantastic life as a husband/father, footballer/restauranteur, and forget about me after I leave.

"What is going on in that large brain of yours?" he teases,

squeezing my hand. "Your forehead looks like the river when the wind is blowing."

"Thanks."

"Are you going to tell me?"

"No. It's personal."

"I tell you everything."

"You do not. You've never told me about Izzy's mom."

He stares deep into my eyes. "Come, I'll show you something."

"That field over there is where I learned to play football." He points to a grassy lot right behind a line of trees, deftly changing the subject.

"This is where it all began, huh?" I go along for a moment. "Where Salvador Torres went from local footballer to Portugal's champion and now a worldwide legend."

He laughs. "Something like that. I was playing with a junior team before you were born."

"I'm almost twenty-two."

"And I'm twenty-nine. I was the youngest player to ever make the Juniors League."

"I didn't know you were such an old man," I tease.

He stares out across the field. "There were plenty of ups and downs. It wasn't all butterflies and rainbows."

"I guess that's true for everyone. Can you tell me what happened with Izzy's mother?"

He groans. Covers his face with his sexy hands. "Not now. Please. I don't want to spoil our moment here."

Part of me feels like it's none of my business because I am not in a romantic relationship with him.

The other part wonders if I'm not letting myself like him more because he's not talking about it.

"Okay," I say finally.

It's difficult figuring out if it's a boundary he's drawn that I must respect. Or if it's a wall he's put up out of habit.

I recognize the strategy.

I thought keeping my mental health issues to myself was a healthy boundary. Until I realized it was a way to keep my family in the dark. Which kept *me* in the dark.

Secrets are horrible stress, and unnecessary when you have a loving family to help ease that pain.

"So, are you going to show me your town, or are we going to stand around admiring the origin of your athletic stardom?"

"Feisty," he says, with a twinkle in his eye.

"Trying to get this show on the road. You promised me a real tour from a local." I side-eye him.

I can't tell what he's thinking but there's a gleam in his eye and before I know it, he picks me up in one motion and flips me over his shoulder.

"Old man, eh?" he smacks my butt as I hang upside down.

He walks past the pool, past the olive trees edging the driveway, and straight to his red sports car.

"Let me down, let me down!" I laugh. "I'm going to throw up my breakfast."

He chuckles, "Nice try, baby. We're here." He leans over and slides my butt into his open convertible red sports car. I land on the cushioned seat, facing forward.

He bends over and kisses my forehead with a loud smack.

"You're welcome."

"Caveman much?" I ask.

"My ancestors were cavemen who lived right here in these hills and valleys," he says. "I can take you to the Prehistoric Rock Art sites."

I stare dumbfounded. "Doesn't mean you can't evolve."

He spreads his arms wide and smiles. "This is me, baby. Take it or leave it." He frowns. "Actually, you better take it."

I grin. "I'll think about it."

Chapter Forty-Two

Izzy wants to stay at the Quinta with Sangria and her grandparents.

She runs out to the car and swings on my door handle. "We want to stay here and play in the garden."

Salvador looks conflicted. I hear him asking his mother if she has plans for the day.

"No, you two go ahead. Izzy will stay with us."

"Are you sure?" Salvador asks. "You've had her all week."

"Hugo, please go." Mrs. Torres hands him a large picnic basket that looks like it could feed a family of five. "I made you guys a little something," she says.

"Take Corrine to the town on the hill with the view you love and show her our world."

He kisses his mom on her cheek.

I wave to Mrs. Torres and pat Izzy's hand, as she tiptoes to see inside the car. "Take care of my baby," I tell her.

Arf! Sangria barks.

"I will," Izzy says struggling to pick up the growing puppy. "He's safe with me."

"Thank you," I say seriously. "You're his Auntie Izzy."

She grins. "I am?"

"Yes, of course. You were there from day one of his life with us."

She smiles and I see a new space where she's lost a tooth recently. Like Sangria, Izzy is growing and changing fast.

I wonder how her mom could not be a part of her life. I mean, where is she? Salvador has only said she's still alive.

Izzy hugs and kisses her father quickly. She wants to go back to playing with the puppy.

"I've been demoted," he grumbles, as he swings his entire body effortlessly into the driver's side of the car.

"Who's Hugo?" I ask as soon as we're on our way.

"Me, it's my first name. Salvador is my second name. But don't ever call me that."

"Why not, *Hugo*?"

He rolls his eyes. Reaches over to take my hand.

"Don't you need both your hands to shift gears up and down all these hills?" I ask.

"Uh-uh." He demonstrates his finesse by driving with one hand by shifting the gear stick with his muscled thigh.

I would swoon if I were Bridget. I burst out laughing instead.

"Does that work on the girls?" I ask when I stop laughing.

"Yes. It's not working on you?"

"Nah, I prefer men who can change gears with their minds."

He lets out a hoot of laughter and puts both hands on the steering wheel. "I'm acting like a teenager, aren't I?"

"A cute one though," I acquiesce.

"I'll keep my hands on the wheel. But just so you know. I'm mentally touching you."

"Oh, that's not creepy at all."

"Baby, I'm so happy I get to spend the day with you."

He's not shy about expressing his feelings, which I admire. I need to learn how to express my deeper feelings. I turn my body to face him.

"I'm thrilled to be here with you. There's nowhere I'd rather be." I wait a beat then add. "And no one I'd rather be with."

I sink back into my seat. That wasn't so hard, right? So why does my heart feel as if a bowling ball rolled right over it?

"I'm glad to hear that, baby." Salvador checks his mirror, reverses fast down a road, then spins the car around like a stuntman.

We come to a stop at a lookout with a vista of the river, bridges, and boats below.

He leaps out and opens my door. My breath is still playing catch up in my lungs.

I can't help but notice that Salvador is a true gentleman. There's so much to like, even love, about him.

But I still don't know the important details. Who is Izzy's mother? Where she is. The not knowing scares me.

His secrets are a warning sign that I'd better pay heed to.

That was always the red flag I ignored in my past relationships.

When the guys were closed off, there was always something risky or menacing, or even undiagnosed, lurking beneath the surface. And that secret always tore us apart eventually.

I can't do that with Salvador. I've been there, done that.

Chapter Forty-Three

After admiring the views and dipping into the picnic basket for a small snack we're back on our sightseeing adventure.

Salvador drives for miles past fields of cows and horses, tractors, and olive trees. We begin to climb up higher and cross a valley to reach a road that meanders with a mind of its own.

Across the terraced hillsides, the port companies have stenciled their names in large black letters on their Quintas' walls.

Every so often, there'd be a lookout to stop and take pictures at. Informative boards described the people, the landscape, and the history of the region.

I make Salvador stop at each one and I read them all.

I read about the peasants who came from miles around to work the land at harvest time.

I learn that this valley is the ancient home to prehistoric tribes and one of the oldest wine-producing regions in the world.

"We even had dinosaurs," Salvador stresses, drawing their images in the dirt with a stick at one stop. "I've seen the rock art and fossils of the old creatures that walked the land."

"Incredible," I say. "Dinosaurs walked here, thousands of years ago in this valley?"

"Yup."

"And look, here's another one." I tiptoe and kiss his cheek as he stands up.

We're giggling like two kids on a playground as he swings the car down a narrow lane off the main road.

We enter a tiny village where the central square is more like a triangle with a very old stone church sitting at the top of the triangle.

We park and stroll about.

Salvador tells me that the houses are constructed with chunky granite blocks from the area. Our Quinta and most of the Quintas around the Douro Valley are built with the same stone."

"Cool."

A fountain in the middle of the triangle spouts freshwater from which I can fill up my water bottle.

Villagers sit on stone seats around the fountain. Some play chess. Others chat in a neighborly fashion.

I'm fascinated by what it must be like to live in a village of only a few hundred people. To know everyone and they know you.

A sign with a book etched in it catches my eye.

I decipher the Portuguese words and read them twice to make sure I understand.

"Salvador," I say, calling him over after he's finished signing autographs for two young fans.

"This is interesting. One of your country's greatest writers of the 20th century was from this village."

"Really?" he asks. "Now *that* I didn't know."

"Oh, you knew the dinosaurs lived here but not this critically acclaimed author of legendary works?"

He put a hand to his chin. "Nope."

"He was nominated several times for the Nobel Prize in Literature."

Salvador's eyes open wide. "Oh, that's big."

"Humongous. And what's crazy is that I've never heard of him!"

"Oh," Salvador lets out a sigh. "I thought it was just me."

I ignore him. "But *I* should have heard about him. *I* should have read at least one of his works."

"Let's ask the villagers. I mean, the man's statute is standing right here." Salvador approaches a few villagers sitting on benches. Most of them shake their heads no. They don't know much about him.

But finally, Salvador asks an older man whose face lights up. "Of course, I know him," he says. "He's famous up here. He wrote about the peasants. How hard they worked the land. He's one of us."

Salvador and I sit on either side of the old man as he reminisces. "He died recently. Only twenty-five years ago."

"Before I was born."

"I was born though," Salvador says. "This is not ancient history."

The old man nods in agreement. "You could say that to discover Miguel Torga's poetry, essays, books, and diary is to be born anew."

"Why do you say that?" I ask cautiously so I don't offend the man.

"Read his last book, *Tales from the Mountain*. His stories are all about this land and his people, the peasant farmers. He describes the region as a paradise lost."

I glance around the triangle. The peace and tranquility of the village, interrupted only by the ringing church bells.

"It looks like a paradise lost," I whisper.

The old man beams at me. "Too bad most people who stop here prefer the bar and beer to the writer and his wisdom."

I clasp my hands around my knees and lean backward so I can get a bigger picture view of the village.

"I'm here for all of it. I just wish I'd read some of his works so I could understand where I am right now even better."

Chapter Forty-Four

Sitting at the bar with my tall handsome footballer sipping a glass of wine, the idea comes to me.

I plunk my glass very hard onto the bar counter.

Salvador snaps to attention, almost tipping over his tiny glass of port. "What's wrong, honey?"

I wave a hand in front of my face. "Nothing. I'm thinking."

To his credit, he doesn't ask any more questions. He lets me sit there, quietly unraveling the layers in my mind.

"I'll be back." I jump off my stool and walk outside into the sunshine. I circle the fountain and gaze at the mountains, my eyes following the birds soaring in the sky.

Finally, I make my way back to the bar and slide onto the stool next to Salvador.

"Are you ready to talk about it?" He asks.

"This may sound crazy, but I want to write a book."

Salvador's eyes open wide. He watches me closely.

"I'm serious. Why can't I?"

He blinks. "Of course, you're going to write a book."

"I can do it."

"And you will do it."

I can tell his words are sincere by the way his eyes lock onto mine. There's no phoniness there.

My idea of writing a book is like finding gold in the least expected place.

And Salvador's happiness at my idea even if he knows nothing about it is even better.

"What's your book going to be about?" He signals for the bill. The barman waves him away. "You don't pay Mr. Torres. Just score a goal in the big game next week."

Salvador laughs. "I will. Just for you."

We walk outside and Salvador pulls my sweater up on my shoulders. I glance at him under my lashes. "Thanks."

I love the way he takes care of me. I wonder for a moment what being his girlfriend would be like. Would it be easy like this? Or would I have to deal with swarms of women vying for his attention?

"Well, do you know what you want to write about?" Salvador's hand is on my lower back as he guides me toward the car.

"About the Douro Valley's literary icon Miguel Torga. And how this beautiful land inspired him. And I'm going to write it in Portuguese." I say that last part defiantly. As if I expect him to protest.

He stops. "His life story? That's wonderful, Corrine. I want to read it already."

"There'll be a lot to research. So much to learn. I'll have to come back to this village and try to follow Torga's trajectory."

"Ah!" Salvador claps his hands. "Finally something I can help with."

"Help how?"

He shakes his keys in the air. "I have a family home nearby. I have a car."

"Several cars," I interrupt.

He grins. "I'll be your literary facilitator. And a financial supporter of the arts. Mr. Torga is from my home region. I want Isabel to grow up and know about him."

"What about you?" I tease. "Don't you want to read about him?"

"Let's not spoil the plan."

"This could work. I will write a biography."

"I bet the schools here will teach it."

"You can be my inspiration," I tease. "I'll translate it myself into English.

He shakes his head. "You amaze me, woman. No wonder I never want you out of my sight."

A warm glow comes over me. "Who says you have to?" I tease.

We reach his car and Salvador hands me a bottle of sparkling water from the cooler in his trunk. "How did you have this revelation? That you must write a book about Miguel Torga?"

I take a sip of my bubbly water and think about the writers' group. Salvador's holding open the car door for me, so I slip in and settle back on the cushion.

"You may as well know," I say as he closes the door.

He slides into his car seat and turns to face me. "Know what?"

I'm almost distracted by his handsome face.

"You were sort of right about the writers and poets' group. I'm not having much luck convincing them to take a chance on me translating their works. I'll just write my own."

"Those pretentious fools," he says, clenching his hand around the gear shift. He glances over with fire in his eyes. "You want me to handle them for you?"

This time it's my eyes that open wide. "Handle them? What on earth does that mean?"

He chuckles. "Nothing, darling. I know some people."

I clear my throat as he zooms out of the village. We head down toward the river gleaming in the distance. "I presume you mean you know someone in the Literature and Translations department at Porto University?"

He doesn't answer.

'Right?" I cover his hand with mine.

He growls. "Let's just say I'll be coming to your next meeting with you."

"Salvador Torres!"

"Corrine Walker!"

"You'd better be joking. Life isn't a football field. You can't go around kicking your opponents."

"I don't *kick* my opponents." He snaps. "I control the field."

"There's a difference?" I snap back.

"Are we fighting?" Salvador lowers his voice. "Because I'm sorry if you don't like my methods. But no one is going to make you feel bad about anything. Not as long as I'm around. And I plan to always be around."

I rub his knuckles to loosen his grip on the gear shift. "It's okay. It's fine." I murmur. His hand relaxes under my touch. But his lips remain in a firm thin line.

We drive in silence for a while. I stare out the window wondering how I feel about this man jumping to my defense so quickly and forcefully.

"I'm not used to the overly protective types," I finally say.

"Well, you've been hanging around the wrong types."

That I knew. I just assumed Salvador was the same. Can a bad boy be loving and protective?

"What can I do?" he asks, breaking the silence that was growing as my mind wandered down rabbit holes of past relationships.

"What do you mean?"

"What can I do that would make you feel comfortable and still solve the problem of these jerks preventing you from doing your chosen profession?"

"Ah," I smile at him. "A compromise? Do you do that on the field?"

He chokes out a laugh. "Absolutely not. There is no compromise in scoring goals. Just action, follow through, and win. If you hesitate you lose. If you think too much, you lose. If you don't focus you lose."

"Sounds like life to me," I concede. "My problem is I think a lot."

He squeezes my hand. "More action, less thinking. I can help with that."

I giggle. "I bet you can. But let's stay on topic."

He picks up my hand and kisses my knuckles. "Let's do that. Tell me about those *arseholes*, as my English opponents would say."

"Well, I've been trying to show the writers that I can translate their works. But they have a lot of doubts and some aren't legit."

Salvador shakes his head. I can tell from the way he's biting his bottom lip that he's holding back a few choice words for them.

I smile. "They did me a favor though."

"How so?" He sips his bottle of water while driving, eyes on the road, but his attention is on me.

"If they hadn't made it difficult, I wouldn't have thought of writing a book about Miguel Torga. I was thinking of applying to the University of Porto for my master's degree. Now I have the perfect topic to research and write about."

Salvador's eyes light up. "Yes!"

I grin and gesture outside the car windows. "I Googled him, you know. He published his works himself. He was even arrested for some of his ideas. But he kept writing and publishing. His story is fascinating."

"And you're going to tell it," Salvador says.

"Damn right."

"And I don't have to beat up any puny writers and poets. Or get Sangria to bite their ankles. "

I roll my eyes. "Thank goodness for that!"

Chapter Forty-Five

The little red car zooms around the hills back down across the bridge up some more roads, and into a picturesque small city.

"Is that a castle or a church?" I ask peering out the front windshield into the sky.

"Church," he says. "The castle is over there." He points behind us.

"Of course, there's a castle." I peer into the distance. "This place has it all."

"Normally people walk the 600-plus steps up to the church as a pilgrimage. But we're going to drive around the back road and get there in no time."

"That's cheating," I howl.

"No. It's practical. I'm hungry. It's time to eat our picnic."

When we're seated next to the church on a soft blanket munching on the goodies packed by Salvador's mom, I concede he had a point.

"Very practical," I admit between bites of the ham and cheese sandwiches. "What's the name of this town."

"Lamego. It's my favorite."

"It feels like a fairytale."

"We'll drive to the castle next. Then you can pretend you *are* in a fairy tale."

"You'd be the Prince Charming?"

He raises an eyebrow. "Who else?"

I choke on my sandwich. "I don't know. A knight? Who wins his lady's hand?" I wave a hand in the air in as regal a manner as possible.

Salvador sticks a tart in my flailing hand.

"I think my mother loves you. She never gives me tarts."

"I love your mother. I love your whole family."

"What about me?"

I smile and pop the tart in my mouth. I lean my head back to see the church behind us.

Everything about this moment feels right. I am where I'm supposed to be. This man. This beautiful town. This delicious feast.

"The verdict is still out on you," I tell him after I finish chewing.

"Out where?" he asks.

"With the angels," I point to the statues around us. "They're weighing your pros and cons."

"Ha! The angels love me. I come here often."

I get serious. "Even if I did love you . . ."

"Which you do."

I roll my eyes. "How could we make this work?"

"What do you mean? If you love me and I love you then it's going to work."

"No, Salvador. It's not that simple. Long distance will never work."

"Who said anything about long distance?" His eyebrows dance into his hairline. "You just said you're staying here to work on your master's degree."

"If I get approved."

"Oh you will," he says with certainty.

"What about after that? You live here. I live across the ocean.

The distance is too much. The world is too big. Why start something that has to end anyway?"

"The world is not that big Corrine that you could leave me and I would never see you again. The world is not so big that I could not find you and be by your side. The world is not so big that I would ever lose you no matter where you are. The world is just not that big."

He says all of that while packing up our picnic. As if his words aren't the most important words I've ever heard in my life.

I can't argue with this man's confidence and commitment. It is so much more than I expected.

Or experienced.

"Now I see why you score all those goals. You don't give up." I try to keep it casual.

He reaches for me across the blanket. Pulls me in his arms. "And I never will."

A cynical part of me thinks this is too good to be true.

And you know what they say about things that are too good to be true.

They probably aren't.

But no matter how much time I spend with Salvador Torres, alone or with his daughter and family, this hunky footballer has not let me down.

But no one is perfect. And the part of me that knows bad things do happen is waiting for the first shoe to drop.

Chapter Forty-Six

The next day, on our way back to Porto, Izzy rides in the tiny backseat with Sangria next to her.

Aunt Esmeralda follows us in her car.

Salvador takes the scenic route again. Along the way, he tells us football stories that the press would love to know.

Stories about how he and a few of his teammates have an ongoing Monopoly game they play late at night at their hotels during their away games.

"And here I thought you guys went out clubbing. You're ruining your image with Monopoly."

"We play for real money."

"Oh," I say. "Well, that's different. Don't lose."

"I won't," he assures me.

Izzy falls asleep with Sangria nestled in her arms.

"Good, she needs a nap. My stories work all the time," he says with a look of satisfaction.

"You're a great dad," I tell him.

"She's a great kid."

When we stop for gas, Salvador heads inside the station to pay. Izzy wakes up and we take Sangria over to the grassy lot to do his business.

Izzy slips her hand in my free one. Her small fingers curl around mine. "Are you going to marry my daddy?"

I freeze. "What?"

"Are you and Daddy going to get married? My friend at school is going to her mother's wedding. She has a fairy dress with diamonds. I want to wear a fairy dress too."

"Ah," I say slowly. "A fairy dress. I love fairy dresses too. Maybe we can find one for you as a special gift." I feel I've handled Izzy's out-of-the-blue question well.

Then she pipes up, "But are you going to marry Daddy?"

I can't pretend I don't understand.

While Sangria is walking in circles looking for the exact spot that he needs, I use that time to ask her. "Why do you ask that, Izzy?"

She swings our hands high. "Because I *want* you to marry my daddy."

I look at this little girl who does not have a mother. She has a father who adores her and an extended family. But like me, she has no mother.

Her large eyes seem to grow larger as she stares at me. Waiting for my answer.

I swallow a lump in my throat. She reminds me of my little sisters, Daisy and Emerald. They were Izzy's age when our Mom died.

"Well, are you?" Izzy drags me out of my memory reel.

"I don't know," I say honestly. "I never thought about marrying anyone."

"But you love my dad, right?"

"Who doesn't love him?" I ask, stalling.

Izzy frowns at me.

Oh dear. This avoiding a question never worked on Daisy and Emerald either.

I'm about to confess that I think I do love her dad when he walks up, concern in his eyes.

"You guys look like you're in the middle of a serious conversation."

"You have no idea," I mutter to myself.

I look around to check on Sangria.

Izzy does not let go of my hand. It's not easy to hold her hand, Sangria's leash, and the poop bag all at the same time.

When we return to the car, Izzy releases my hand and runs to her father. He swings her little body up in one hand.

He opens his other arm wide. I step toward them and all three of us plus Sangria are now in a family group hug.

It doesn't feel awkward. It feels like something I need.

"I take it Izzy told you about the pirate party that we're having at Sangria Nights this weekend? Well, next weekend."

"No, she did not tell me about a pirate party." I give Izzy my meanest stare.

She giggles and smacks a little hand over her face. "I forgot about that. I told her about something better."

"What's better than pirate costumes?" he asks with a fake shocked look.

"Please don't say it," I beg silently.

She crosses her arms. "Fairy dresses."

Salvador twists his mouth. "Okay, if you say so."

He buckles her into the back seat. "But please tell me. I hate surprises."

"You're not supposed to say 'hate.'" She waggles a finger at him.

I smile at the way Izzy fearlessly tells off her father.

The rest of the way home the conversation is about the pirate party, which he and Danielo started years ago when they bought the restaurant.

"Pirate crews from nearby villages invade the restaurant's patio. They arrive on boats, pull out their swords, and compete in drinking games."

"You're joking."

He shakes his head. "Nope. Some even have to walk the plank."

"And fall into the cold water?" I shiver.

Izzy giggles from the back seat. "They get saved before they walk all the way off."

"Thank goodness. It sounds like a movie. Is there a pirate booty to capture?"

Salvador chuckles. "Indeed. We have sponsors who donate prizes."

Izzy squeals. "The prizes are the best."

"The pirates have to bid on the prizes. The money goes to charity." Salvador shifts gears and glances at me. "Every penny. We supply the alcohol. Organize the scavenger hunt and games."

I'm honestly impressed. Any man who can throw a pirate party to raise money for charity is a keeper.

When we arrive in Porto, Salvador drops me off first. He's taking Izzy home to tuck her in, then coming back to my apartment.

"We'll go out to dinner to celebrate," he says. "You're writing a book. You're doing your master's degree here. And you *love* me."

I laugh as I wave goodbye to them and head upstairs.

An hour later, I'm sitting on the sofa, showered and wearing my most comfy PJs.

When Salvador walks in that's where he finds me reading a book.

"I just want to sit here for the rest of the evening."

"Perfect," he says stretching out his long legs next to me. He slides my head onto a pillow on his lap and strokes my hair as I read.

When I tell him it's okay to turn on the TV, he finds a football game to watch and that's how we stay for the rest of the evening.

Every once in a while, I glance up from my book and stare at his chiseled chin.

"I can get used to this," he says.

I slide my bookmark into my book, close it, and cuddle against his chest. Both of his arms wrap around me instantly.

"Me too," I whisper.

His hand strokes my shoulder. I look up to find his lips mere inches from mine.

When he finally presses his mouth against mine, I inhale sharply.

Our kiss lasts much longer than before. It's followed by another and another until I can't breathe.

He kicks off his shoes and slides his body down the length of the couch, his long legs hanging off the edge. We're facing each other, staring into each other's eyes.

"You surprise me. Every single day." My fingers play with the buttons on his pullover sweater. "Thank you for a beautiful day."

He sits up and in one swift move yanks off his sweater and tosses it across the room.

I stare in wonder at the solid dips and planes of his chest muscles.

Looking further south, I can't help but notice the terraced vineyards of the Duoro Valley have nothing on his serrated abdominal muscles.

"Wow," I mutter, running my hand over his ripped abs. "Those underwear ads don't lie." I'm referring to billboards I've seen of him wearing only a pair of briefs. I'd presumed his body was airbrushed. "For once, reality matches the fantasy."

He pulls me close to his bare chest. "Hush, so I can kiss you again."

And he does so with the same passionate, all-consuming heat as our first kiss in Athens. As if he's picking up where he left off.

Under his tongue, I lose track of time. My book falls off the couch and I don't retrieve it. Nothing in my life compares to this man and his wonderful arms wrapped around me.

Later, as I fall asleep in his arms I feel as if I'm being rocked to the lullaby my mother used to sing to me when I was small.

Something about teddy bears in the woods and picnics and disguises.

Chapter Forty-Seven

Salvador is away all week, playing football in Germany and then Italy, but he'll be back for the pirate party on Saturday.

He's been phoning, sending me flowers, and even pastries are delivered to my door. Like he thinks I may forget about him while he's away.

As if!

I haven't told him about my past eating disorder. I don't want him to think he can't send me pastries.

Besides, writing in my journal helps me keep track of my mental health. Which in turn helps me stay focused on self-care.

After promising myself and my sisters to be vigilant, I won't let anything or anyone take me to that remote cave in my mind ever again.

This is why I drag Carlos to another writers' club meeting at the usual cafe.

"I have to stay relevant," I tell him. "And I like hearing everyone's ideas. Even if they don't include me. I can't let their rejection define me."

"Their loss," he says in solidarity. "The meetings have some benefits so we'll keep attending."

"Exactly," I say. "Let's participate anyway. Everyone won't love us in life, doesn't mean we run away."

He laughs. "Everyone loves *me*."

I smack his arm. "Of course, you're a fantastic artist. You bring beauty to the world."

He doodles a quick sketch of me with hearts over my head. I'm trying not to laugh out loud and listen to the debate going on about politics in fiction.

Do you want to go to a party this weekend?" I whisper.

His head pokes up like a turtle out of a shell. "A party?" He sounds suspicious.

I feel a bit guilty that we haven't done anything outside of school stuff. And I want him to know I consider him a friend.

"Yes, a party. You sound like I'm asking you to go to Hades."

He smothers a laugh. We get a few frowns.

One of the members is reading his work aloud so we stay quiet and pay attention.

When the reading is over, Carlos whispers, "What kind of party?"

"Pirate-themed. You could be Blackbeard." I smile hopefully.

He snorts. "Oh, the worst pirate ever?" he asks.

"No, the most famous."

He watches me for a moment. Assessing me somehow.

It's a bit awkward trying to stay in a friend zone with someone who likes you for more than a friend, but thankfully we connect through our mutual love for books and art.

"I'm serious, Carlos, would you like to come to a party at Sangria Nights? You have to dress up. We'll have a good time." I lower my voice. "It'll be more fun than this."

"Anything is more fun than this," he grimaces. "I only come to keep you company."

"And I thank you. So, you'll come?"

"Fine," he says, at the same time we get hushed by the members in front of us.

"Cool," I say. I made a note to tell Salvador that I've invited a friend.

I quickly forget because, on top of classes, tutoring Izzy, and taking care of little Sangria, I have to find a pirate costume for myself.

The night before the pirate party, I'm still costume-less. There was simply no time to shop. Anything I found online would not get here in time.

I find myself knocking on Sylvia's door Friday evening, carrying a bag of pastries to bribe her with. She must have something I can wear in that fancy closet of hers.

My neighbor lets me in with a huge smile on her face.

"What's going on?" I ask. "You look like the proverbial cat that swallowed a . . ."

She puts a finger to her lips and points towards her bedroom.

I gasp. "Which one? You naughty woman."

"The one and only."

"Frank?" I mouth because I don't want to presume and say the wrong name aloud.

She beams. "Of course Frank. The love of my life since I was seventeen."

"I'm so happy for you," I whisper. "I can come back later."

She shakes her head and leads me to the kitchen. I perch on a tall chair and watch her make coffee.

"Do you need me to babysit Sangria for you?" she asks, putting my pastries on a plate along with some of her homemade bread and a full circle of Serra da Estrela cheese.

My stomach growls loudly. "I'm shameless. I can't say no to your delicious bread. And that cheese! It's so rich, ripe and tangy."

Sylvia hands me a cheese knife and I dig in.

In between chewing I mumble, "I came to invite you and . . . *Frank* to Sangria Nights' annual pirate party this weekend."

She claps her hands like a little girl. "Oh, I love the pirate parties. I was already planning on going. I figured you were going too since you're dating the owner."

"Well, I'm not *dating* him. Not officially." But as I hear myself I stop. Who am I kidding?

"As we say in this country, 'To a good listener, half a word is enough.'"

"What does that mean?"

"It means, you don't have to explain. You've said enough."

I lean forward and smell the fresh flowers sitting in an ornate vase on her table.

"To a keen observer, half a flower is enough."

It's her turn to smack my arm. "He brought them yesterday."

"And you thanked him?" I grin.

"I waited over forty years for him. I give new meaning to the phrase, 'An ounce of patience is worth a pound of brains.'"

I reach over and hug her. "I'm very happy for you. And you found him on a dating app after all these years."

"Let's make sure it doesn't happen to you. Don't lose the man you love the first time around. Now how can I help you?"

I clear my throat. "Do you have anything that I can wear to the pirate party? I was thinking . . . "

Before I can finish my thought Sylvia leaps up. "Do I ever. I have a lot of retired wench clothing."

I frown. "What?"

"Wait here."

Sylvia returns from her bedroom with her arms full of shiny, fringed, sexy outfits. Most of them don't look appropriate in more ways than one.

When we've sorted through the possible combinations, I end up with an outfit that'll make Salvador's jaw drop.

A very short skater skirt, a white peasant blouse that exposes my shoulders, black fishnet stockings, high heels, and a red swirly silk scarf that wraps around my waist, tying it all together literally and figuratively.

"Thanks to you, not only will Salvador's eye pop out but Carlos will be shocked."

"You invited Carlos?" Her eyebrows shoot up. "Is there a love triangle going on with you, him, and Salvador?"

"*Noooo,*" I stress, a bit too loudly. "Carlos is a friend."

Sylvia pats my hand. "It's probably nothing," she says. "But I sense that Salvador is a bit . . . ." She twists her mouth.

"A bit what?" I ask the question, but I think I already know the answer.

"Protective," she echoes my thoughts.

I don't respond, but she may be right.

"I hope that inviting Carlos won't be a problem. Because he's my friend. I want everyone to get along. Besides, it's a party."

"A *pirate* party," Sylvia specifies.

"Right," I mumble on my way out. "What can go wrong?"

Chapter Forty-Eight

The party is in full swing when Sylvia, Frank, and I arrive on Saturday night. I've left little Sangria at home in his crate with a new bone to chew on.

I haven't seen Salvador as yet because he and Danielo were at *Sangria Nights* all day, setting up and organizing the event.

I texted him and offered to help out but he turned me down.

He said he wanted me to have the full magical experience. Which I wouldn't have if I saw all the hard work that went into transforming the restaurant into a pirate's lair.

I appreciated his wish for me to fall under his pirate spell, but I missed him badly.

When we walk in, I don't see him anywhere.

But then again, I wouldn't recognize him because everyone is dressed in pirate gear, and an actual Jolly Rogers ship with a Cross and Bones flag is tied up next to the restaurant's large deck.

"Whoa! Look at that," I exclaim. "A bit overboard, no?"

Sylvia giggles. "Punny."

Sylvia and Frank take selfies in front of the large vessel, while I scan the dock for my special pirate.

I had heard that there would be some traditional boats involved, but I didn't expect three beautiful Portuguese boats, wooden barrels on their decks, and pirate crews brandishing swords to be part of the decor.

It was all storybook perfect.

"I can see why they raise as much money as they do," I shout to Sylvia.

It's too loud to talk and a bit chilly so we head back inside away from the noise and din of the pirates recreating their own *Pirates of the Caribbean* scenes.

Then, the most handsome pirate of them all walks toward us from the deck. I'm staring mesmerized.

Is that a real parrot on his shoulder? I'm asking myself. It sure looks real.

When he reaches my side, the parrot squawks loudly.

Salvador slips it a snack and pets the ruffled feathers.

His white billowy shirt does not hide the firm muscular lines of his body if anything, it accentuates them.

Tight, black britches hug his legs like a second skin. A sword sits on his hip in a scabbard.

Shiny black boots are laced up his calves and a black patch covers one of his eyes, completing the image.

"If anyone here looks like a pirate, it is you, Salvador Torres," I shout over the music.

He goes behind the bar and pours me a glass of sangria, adding fresh lime and orange slices to the already fruit-laden drink.

He comes around to my side of the bar and takes my hand twirling me around so he can check out my outfit.

"Sylvia did her magic," I shout.

"No, she added to *your* magic."

He twirls me around again and pulls me into his arms. "I missed you, baby."

I'm still clutching my glass of sangria.

All of a sudden, the parrot sticks his long beak down and sucks on my straw. I freeze.

I'm so afraid to move I just let him drink.

Salvador is talking to someone over my shoulder and doesn't notice.

The parrot raises his head and eyes me with dark beady orbs as if to say, "Your turn."

I don't know whether to laugh or step back or what.

"Uhm . . . Salvador?"

"Yes, sweetheart?"

I hand him my drink. "Can I get a new one, please? Your parrot had his way with mine."

Salvador fake scolds his parrot. "Naughty Oliver." He goes to get me a new drink and I shake my head laughing. Wait until I tell my sisters.

It takes Salvador a while to get me a new drink. With every step he takes someone stops to hug him, kiss his cheeks, or congratulate him on this party.

It gives me a chance to watch him interact with others. The smooth way he moves his larger-than-life body so smaller men and women don't feel blocked or overshadowed.

The joy lighting up his face is contagious. Everyone he greets returns his broad smiles.

Salvador may look like a real-life pirate but he has a heart of gold.

How else could he have rescued Sangria from the animal shelter? And the way he raises his daughter to be confident and fearless?

And the way he makes me feel loved and adored even from another country.

He returns to my side with a fresh glass of sangria and leads me away to a quiet space outside the party area. "Your ale me fair lass."

"And what may your name be pirate King?"

"Laurens de Graff, at your Service."

I raise an eyebrow.

"Who is Laurens de Graaf?" I ask. "I never heard of this pirate, sir."

"Lassy, this here is a pirate you should know about."

"Why, my pirate King?"

"Because he was a respected Black Dutch pirate who had been enslaved by the Spanish and forced to work on a plantation in the Canary Islands before he became free and started his pirate crew."

"You're making that up."

He shakes his head hard and Oliver squawks."

"No, look it up. de Graaf ended up in your country. Working with the French in Biloxi, Mississippi."

I've found that the truth is always in the details. And Salvador is giving a lot of details.

"Tell me more," I urge, sipping my drink and keeping it far from Oliver.

"Well, the historians described him as a tall, handsome, white man with blond hair."

"Interesting," I say. "Not many pirates were described in such detail."

"Exactly."

"The truth can also be hidden by excessive details," I muse.

"I think they didn't want anyone to know that a Black man could inspire thousands of followers. Anyway, he targeted the Spanish ships. Probably because of his being enslaved by them."

He tips his head at me. "Captain Laurens de Graaff at your service. I am only taking on his persona to enlighten the public about his existence. I was interviewed by the press earlier. They didn't believe me so I imagine they will be researching Mr. de Graaf tonight."

I stare with my eyes wide open at Salvador.

"What?"

"Why do you always surprise me? Every time I think you're a cocky but nice jock, you go and do something like this."

"Like what?" He lifts his hands and smooths the hair around my face. His palms rest on my shoulders. "I want to kiss you but I'm afraid Oliver might object."

"Like raise money for charity and change history at the same time."

He smiles. "It's how I win. I keep them guessing."

I must admit, he's right.

We leave our sheltered space and head back into the melee.

Salvador spends the rest of the evening socializing and introducing me to friends and teammates.

My head starts to spin as I get overwhelmed by the loud music, flashing lights, and sparkly costumes, not to mention the sangria.

I leave his side and step away to get a breather. It is while doing so that I see Carlos walk in looking like the most handsome, swashbuckling real-life Black pirate I've ever seen.

Not that I've seen any. Salvador doesn't count as he's trying to enlighten people and change history.

I rush to grab Carlos's arm so I don't lose him. "Who are you supposed to be?" I pant.

"I'm Black Ceasar. The best Black pirate of the Caribbean."

"Hmmm . . . you may have competition there." I relay the story of Laurens da Graaf to him.

"Oh, the pirate who died in America?"

"How does everyone know these things and I don't?" I sulk.

Carlos smiles. "I hope there's a lot in this world still to learn."

"Thank you for coming to the party. I don't know many people here."

"Thank you for inviting me."

"Excuse me, we haven't met." Salvador is beside me, but Oliver is no longer perched on his shoulder.

I drop Carlos' arm and step back.

I introduce the two pirates proudly to each other.

Salvador stares at my hands that had just been clinging to Carlos. Like there's blood on them.

"Nice to meet you." Carlos extends a hand to Salvador. I sense that Salvador is taking deep breaths. As if to calm himself. But why?

Carlos' hand hangs in the air for a little too long before Salvador reaches over and shakes it.

"Welcome to the party," he says. But his voice lacks the same warmth he showed to others.

I poke him in his side, but his eyes are smoldering. Like how Sangria looks when a much bigger dog approaches us during our walks.

But why would Salvador need to show fear or distrust? I don't figure it out because someone calls Salvador and he excuses himself.

"So that's the Jaguar," Carlos says.

I feel embarrassed at how Salvador acted.

"I'm sorry," I tell Carlos. "Let's get a drink."

We find Sylvia and I introduce Carlos to her and Frank.

We grab sangria glasses from a passing waiter.

"That's the guy you're seeing?" Carlos asks casually.

"Yes, but I've never seen this side of him."

That's not true. I saw it in Athens when his best friend hugged me. I ignored it then.

"He doesn't look happy that I'm here," Carlos observes.

"Let's go outside and see the band," I say. "It's a party."

I'll ignore Salvador's weird behavior and have fun. Maybe I was imagining it.

We head out to the deck where the band is playing merengue and salsa songs. People are twirling, spinning, and enjoying the cool night air.

The dance area is crowded. I'm happy to tap my foot and sway my hips.

"By the way, I love your costume," Carlos says taking a sip of his sangria. "You look even more beautiful than usual."

If my blush could show up on my dark skin, I'd be bright red.

"Thank you," I say. "You look amazing. But I think I told you that already."

Sylvia comes up and speaks into my ear," Hey sweetheart, we're going to leave now."

I smile at Sylvia. "I'm having a good time. I'll stay longer."

"Don't forget your man," Sylvia whispers. "He's sulking in the corner."

I look at where her eyes direct me to.

Sure enough, Salvador is talking to one of his teammates, but his gray eyes are on me. And they look like thunderclouds.

"Okay, thanks."

Carlos has gone to get new drinks. I walk over to Salvador. His arm magnetically hooks around my waist. "I missed you," he whispers.

"I'm right there. You haven't taken your eyes off me for a minute."

He shakes his head. "Not for a second."

"What?"

"I didn't take my eyes off you for a second."

The happiness I'm feeling takes a nosedive. I wasn't wrong earlier. Salvador *was* being distrustful.

"Well, maybe you should. All I was doing was talking to a friend."

"A friend who has more than a friendly interest in you."

I can't argue with that.

Chapter Forty-Nine

"Can I talk to you in private?" Salvador asks.

I don't answer, just indicate with my hand to lead the way.

As I pass Carlos in the crowd, I tell him I'll catch him later. He nods and heads back outside.

Salvador shows me to a room down a hallway from the bar area. It's huge, with timbered beams, two couches, and a large dark wooden desk. Glass cabinets hold bottles of liquor in neat rows.

"This used to be a rich merchant's home," Salvador explains, as I take a seat on one of the couches and cross my legs.

Once the door is closed it is remarkably quiet. Almost tomb-like after all the noise and revelry we left behind.

"Very cozy."

Then I remember why we're here. "Too bad."

Salvador sits at the edge of the desk, his hands hanging by his sides. His pirate demeanor looks deflated. His billowy shirt is no longer billowing.

"I'm sorry," he says.

That catches me off guard. I wasn't expecting an apology. As far as I can tell, he felt justified in behaving like a jealous boyfriend.

"For what?"

He looks at me with eyes that are cloudy and gray.

"I felt as if my heart would explode when I saw you in that man's arms. I felt as if you were slipping away from me. I've heard how highly you speak of Carlos."

I focus on my right fishnet stocking leg as I try to make sense of his words.

"You are Porto's golden boy. You're a hero. Everyone loves you. And you're telling me that you're jealous of my classmate? And I wasn't *in* his arms. I was holding his arm."

"Yes."

I fling an armful of hair over one shoulder. I rub my eyes and suck in my bottom lip. "That is madness."

"But it's the truth."

His brutal honesty makes it difficult to be angry.

I suck in some air and take a good look at the man before me. There's a difference in the set of his shoulders. Instead of broad and imposing, they look hunched and sad.

Sympathy for him floods me to the core. He's hurting. Something or rather someone has hurt him badly.

I stand up and walk slowly toward him. Halfway there I kick off my high heels. They're killing my feet after all that dancing.

When I reach him I take his hands in mine.

I kiss his cheek. I place a hand along the side of his face. "It's all in your head. Those are just thoughts. Carlos is my friend. I will always have friends. Some of them will be male. Don't let your mental pictures ruin our reality, please."

He shakes his head and closes his eyes.

"I thought I'd gotten over this."

"What happened to you?" I ask. "To make you think like this?"

His head hangs a little.

Gone is the confident, strong, commanding person, the

athlete, who is the king of the soccer field, the father, who is king of his daughter's heart, and the man whom I'm beginning to fall in love with. Or have fallen in love with.

"Are you going to tell me?" I ask gently.

"It's how I lost Isabel's mother," he says cryptically.

"What do you mean?" I cross my arms on my chest. I remember my therapist's words when dealing with stressful situations. I need to focus and stay calm. These words are my motto.

I can't let myself rush into hugging him and trying to alleviate his fears like I did with all the boys I dated before.

I was always the one who would try to make their lives better even learning a new language to make Ivandro's life easier. Maybe because I couldn't fix myself or didn't know how to that I focused on others.

It never occurred to me to try and make my life easier. Which is why I hold myself back now. To give Salvador a chance to speak.

"What do you mean it is how you lost Isabel's mother?" I repeat.

His eyes are full of pain. He speaks in a low voice. "She swore she loved me. We were supposed to get married and be together forever, but soon after Isabel was born, she found someone else to love. My best friend."

My mind rushes to Danielo.

"Not Danielo. The other man grew up with me, played football with me in school, then married the woman I was supposed to wed."

I blink hard. No wonder he was suspicious and distrustful. He'd been betrayed on multiple levels. I swallow my urge to hug him. I need to ask some hard questions first.

"Oh, that must have been horrible. Do you still love her?"

I want to know but I also don't want to know the answer to that question.

"It's hard not to love the woman who gave me Isabel," he says. "But no, I don't love her in the way you mean."

All the air feels like it's been sucked out of the room. I'm not sure what he's saying.

"What way do you love her?"

My heart clutches at the look in his eyes.

"I don't love her the way I love you," he says. "But I have love for her. More importantly, I feel extremely hurt by her choice to leave me and Isabel." His voice cracks, along with my heart.

I'm not sure falling in love with Salvador is wise.

He may not be a bad boy type, but he's got baggage that makes him as unavailable as the others.

Why do I gravitate towards these men?

I take a deep breath to focus on what's happening right now.

"It's hard to live with someone leaving you like that."

I say it to be comforting. But the truth of this hits hard.

My circumstances are different, but the result is the same.

A person I loved and thought I would have for a lifetime deserted me, too. Even if it wasn't her fault.

Salvador realizes what I'm thinking about because he straightens up and comes over to me. "Hey, your loss was so much greater. I don't want to compare. Mine is over and I have you."

I swipe away the tears threatening to fall. I give a weak smile.

"You know I never got to dance with you," he says. "May I have this dance?" He takes off his sword and lays it on the desk.

"We can't hear the music."

Salvador brushes away my objection and pulls out his iPhone. "What do you want to hear?"

"How about *Drops of Jupiter*?" I ask. "It was my mom's favorite song."

He turns and stares at me. "It's *my* favorite song."

"No way."

He slides open his phone. "Look."

He shows me the first playlist on his phone and there at the top is *Drops of Jupiter*.

"Is it your favorite because of your lost love?" I ask.

"No. This has been *my* song since I was a kid. I used to wonder what drops of Jupiter would look like."

He puts on the song and holds me close. We sway and he spins me. I twirl around and slide back into his arms.

As we dance, he sings every word like it has the most special meaning for him.

If I listen closely, I hear my mom's voice singing along with his.

It's the kind of moment you wish would last forever.

Chapter Fifty

After our heart-to-heart talk and dance, Salvador and I have grown closer together.

That's why when Carlos invites me to join his public mural painting, I jump at the opportunity to go.

But I also text Salvador who has football practice and invite him to stop by afterward. A part of me is hoping we can all be friends.

I grab Sangria's leash and walk to the location. My first reaction is shock. The mural fills up the entire wall of a building. It depicts a larger version of Carlos' rainforest paintings I'd seen in his apartment.

I can see the outlines and shadows of rainforest animals lurking on and under the tree branches.

They're still hidden though. Like they're not ready to be fully recognized or known.

"Wow!" I exclaim. "You did it." I'm standing next to a ladder on which Carlos is perched on the highest rung painting a far corner of the wall.

"I did. But grab a brush and join in. I want everyone to help finish it so it will belong to the community."

I look around at the children with paintbrushes in hand who are spreading paint along the bottom edge of the wall.

Their parents or older siblings point out when they miss a spot. There's a lot of laughter and goofiness happening with the painting.

I step back to see the big picture. It is truly magnificent. A rainforest coming alive in the middle of Porto.

I hesitantly dab my brush into red paint and ask Carlos what to do with it. "Where should I start? What should I paint?"

"First, stop asking what you *should* do. There are no 'shoulds' in painting."

I wipe my free hand on my denim overalls. "Easy for the master to say," I mutter under my breath.

I begin dabbing red paint on emerald green leaves, "creating" flowers. I get caught up in the rhythm of the brush and the red blooms appearing under my hand.

Sangria's leash is tied to a bench rung and he's watching me from under the bench.

"You want to help, too?" I ask him.

Arf! Arf! he barks attracting attention. Soon, kids are all around him petting his head and rubbing his belly.

I shake my head at Sangria, who is acting like no one ever plays with him.

My back begins to hurt. I stand up to stretch only to catch Carlos watching me from on top of his ladder.

"What?" I ask suspiciously. "Am I doing it wrong?"

He wipes away sweat on his brow with the edge of his tee shirt. "There's no wrong way. There's only creating something out of nothing."

"Great. I'm creating a mess out of your hard work."

"Which means you're doing it right. Nothing is perfect right away. Or even after a long time. There's been billions of dollars spent on rockets that failed to get to Mars. That's learning by mistakes. Expensive ones."

"Thank you for comparing my senseless dabbling with a space program."

"You're welcome." He says it firmly. Now get back to making your mess."

I smile and put on my earbuds.

Honestly, I do feel an attraction to Carlos. One built on a foundation of mutual interests. A kindred spirit. Attractions don't always have to be physical, I'm realizing.

And it doesn't take away from the deep feelings I'm developing for Salvador.

After I've painted flowers halfway along the wall, Carlos reappears by my side.

"I'm so glad you came."

"Me too."

He points me to a different part of the mural that needs some TLC. We get to work immediately painting side by side.

I pull out my earbuds and turn up the music on my iPhone. People sing along. Couples dance as their kids paint.

Sangria woofs and wags his tail at every child passing by. I throw back my head loving the freedom I feel surrounded by art, friendship, and beautiful music in my adopted city.

"What's going on here?" A voice pierces my bubbly mood.

I spin around. Salvador is standing at the edge of the sidewalk with a grim look on his face.

His football practice doesn't end until much later, so I'm surprised to see him here.

And equally surprised to hear his question.

"What are you doing here?" I ask confused. "Is everything okay with you? With Izzy?"

He nods curtly. "Yes, everything is okay with me and Izzy. Is everything *fine* with you?" The way he says the word "fine" is like it's the new four-letter word. His eyes are glued to me and Carlos, side by side paintbrushes in hand.

A stinging on my back and shoulders feels like fire ants are attacking me. I pull my sweater sleeves down and peer at Salvador.

His eyebrows are scrunched like curved caterpillars. His hands are curled at his sides. His eyes are the worst. They have a vacant faraway look as if he's somewhere else.

I hurry over to him and place a hand on his chest. "Hey, you're here with me."

I feel as if I must drag him back from the edge of some cliff he's hanging on to.

"Do you like him?" he asks.

"Who? Carlos?" My spine stiffens. "We've been through this already."

"I know." He scrubs a hand across his face. Flattens his hair. Looks at me with wounded eyes.

"I can't do this, Corrine."

My heart sinks. "Do what?" But I think I already know.

"I can't see you with another man and be okay with it. I tried. But it's not working. It's too hard. I can't go through what happened to me and Izzy again. It's torture."

He's looking at me as if I have the power to hurt him more than anyone in the world.

"We're just painting. I'm not going to hurt you, Salvador," I whisper.

He shakes his head. "How do you know that? You can't guarantee that."

I shake my head. "No, I can't."

I drop my hand from his chest. No matter how much I want to, I can't protect Salvador from his demons.

Because for him, I *am* the demon.

I'm the catalyst for his pain now. I'm the reason he's trembling.

This large beautiful, athletic, golden boy of Porto is afraid I will hurt him and nothing I can say will change that.

He looks at the kids who are busy painting. They're ignoring the drama happening under their noses. I'm glad this mural isn't some place the paparazzi hang out.

Then he looks at me, a shroud of pain and sorrow on his face. He closes his eyes as if trying to block out a picture in his mind that is haunting him.

I ache for him. But if there's anything I've learned is that I can't fix people. I can only be supportive of their journeys.

"I have to go now." His voice is bleak. "I'll call you."

He looks at Carlos. "I'm sorry I . . . ."

"It's cool, man," Carlos says stepping forward.

Before I can say anything, Salvador turns and walks away, very fast, almost in a run. Even if I wanted to catch up with him, I couldn't.

I watch his retreating figure until I can't see even the tiniest speck of him.

I cover my mouth with one hand and wrap an arm around myself. I inhale sharply and exhale.

It doesn't make the horrible ache in my gut go away. But it does keep me standing.

I turn around and my eyes latch onto the beautiful mural glowing in the darkening sky. Its stealth animals lurk around the way our shadows and demons hide until something or someone comes along to reveal them.

Carlos is wise enough to give them their space on the wall.

I go over to say good night to him. I feel embarrassed he witnessed that. But grateful he had the grace to be kind to Salvador.

"Corrine," he says gently. "Sometimes the hardest things you have to do will hurt the people you love the most."

"Huh?"

"Think about it. That wasn't easy for him. He has your best interest at heart. I respect the man for telling you what he can't handle."

The truth hits hard.

Salvador Torres has left me.

No matter how I try, no matter what I do, I always get left behind.

Chapter Fifty-One

It's been three days since Salvador showed up at the mural. Three days since he said he'll call but hasn't.

Three days since I got a morning text from him. Or an afternoon heart emoji or sweet pastries or flowers.

Three days is a long time when you love someone and you don't know if they still love you.

I don't even have the excuse of going to his home to tutor Izzy because her school has ended for the holidays and she's at her grandparents' Quinta.

By the fourth day, I'm so despondent I organize a group video call with my sisters. They made me promise to call them if I ever felt bad about anything. So I'm keeping my promise.

"Tell us again exactly what happened," says Ava who is busy making gelato in the background. She's making me wish I was back home sitting at the kitchen counter, taste-testing her delicious frozen treats.

I relay the entire story again from beginning to end.

All of my sisters are online and are paying attention. Emerald is even taking notes, which I would think is funny except nothing feels funny right now.

"This must be so hard for you," says Daisy sympathetically.

"It is," I tell them. "I like him a lot.

"He sounds wonderful in so many ways," says Bridget.

She's outside in the olive grove surrounded by sunshine on the island of Aegina. She's in overalls something I never thought I would see Bridget wearing and she looks completely happy.

It gives me hope that one day I will also find someone like Bridget found Ajax. I thought I had. But now he's disappeared from my life.

I sit back in my chair and turn the tablet so my sisters can see out the window. I want to show them how beautiful Porto is.

I don't want this conversation to be solely about my troubles.

"Are you trying to change the subject?" Ava asks, perceptive as usual.

"No, why do you ask that?" I stall.

"Because as beautiful as Portugal is, I think we're all more concerned about how you're doing there dealing with Salvador and your relationship with him."

"Point taken," I say. "I've never shared the sad stuff with you before."

"No, you haven't," says Emerald. "And you should have because it's far more interesting than what's happening in my high school."

I laugh. "Hey enjoy high school. It's where you can build a good foundation for the kind of partner you'll want as you get older."

"In other words, do as you say, not as you did, right?"

I laugh loudly. "Something like that. But okay if you want me to deep dive into this problem, what am I gonna do about Salvador Torres? I like him a lot. He's perfect in so many ways. I love how he is with his daughter. I love how he is with his mother and father. I love how he is with Sangria and mostly I love how he is with me."

"That's a lot of loves," Bridget says. "I don't know, sis, sounds like you're caught. Hook, line, and sinker."

I drop my head in my hands. "I am in love with him. I don't know what to do."

"Poor guy," says Daisy. "He does sound like he's got some issues but aren't we all damaged? A bit anyway?"

I nod my head. "I am. Or was. I'm in a constant state of healing. Why did I have to meet a guy who's not ready?" I wail.

Daisy, who is knitting a scarf of many colors, looks up, catches my eye, and says, "Since we're all damaged in some way, the real question is what is he doing about it."

Bridget claps her hands. "That's it exactly."

"I don't know the answer to that."

"Do you need me to come to Portugal to spend some time with you?" Bridget asks.

I shake my head fast. "No, I'll be okay."

Ava holds up a piece of paper and waves it at the screen. "Maybe you should make a pros and cons list. That always works for me."

Bridget laughs. "No, it doesn't. Remember how many cons you had for Tyler in Italy and you still ended up with him? And you're still madly in love."

Ava nods. "That's true. The biggest con was our distance and he fixed that right away by deciding to change where he was going to finish his master's degree, and he moved back home."

"For you. He did that for you," says Bridget. "The question is what is Salvador doing for Corrine."

I hurry up and say, "No, no, no. I don't want him to do anything for me. That's not right."

Emerald sticks her nose close to the screen. "Are you kidding? Corrine, how exactly is a man supposed to show you that he'll be there for you?"

"How do you know any of this, little sister? You're only seventeen."

"Going on eighteen," Emerald says, rolling her eyes at me. "And I've had a boyfriend for *months*."

"Don't remind me," Daisy mutters.

No one says anything because we don't like to remember how hard it was for Daisy to be in love with the boy who picked Emerald over her.

"How do we know when it's okay to build a relationship with someone who is suffering and who has issues that are deep-rooted the way Salvador's issues seem to be? How do we know?"

I cringe at the desperate note in my voice. But it's a question I think everyone would love an answer to.

Emerald hits her open notebook with her pen. "You trust your gut, Corrine."

"I'm not sure what it means," I confess. "Under these circumstances."

Daisy puts down her knitting and looks me in the eye. "I just texted Dad and he says that I can come visit you for Christmas. He's looking up tickets right now."

"You're coming to Portugal?" I exclaim. Sangria's head pops up at the high note of excitement in my voice.

Arf!

"You're going to Portugal?" Ava, Bridget, and Emerald echo in disbelief.

"Yes," Daisy says matter-of-factly. "You've never asked for our help ever. We never knew that you needed it but now you're asking for our help." She winks. "Whether you like it or not. I'm coming to help you."

Tears spring to my eyes because it's true. I've never asked my sisters for help.

I see Ava wiping tears from her own eyes. She nods. "Yes, Daisy. This is the right thing to do. We're all here for you, Corrine."

"But why does Daisy get to go to Portugal? I want to go too." Emerald pouts.

Ava hugs Emerald. "Dad and I need you here, sweetie."

"And Jackson," she says, bringing up her boyfriend once again. "I guess it's okay."

"Thank you all for your help," I murmur. "And thank you, Daisy. I can't wait to see you."

It's true. I can't wait to show my little sister Porto's charms. And confide in her in person.

"Are there any cute guys for me in Porto?" Daisy asks.

"I'm going to take you to my favorite bakery. I have a sweet, handsome young man to introduce to you."

"Whoa," says Bridget. "One boyfriend problem at a time please."

We all laugh aloud.

As for me, I'm just happy my sister is coming to spend the holidays with me and Sangria.

Chapter Fifty-Two

Two days later when I've all but given up hope of ever hearing from or seeing Salvador again, he calls to say he just got back to Porto from a couple of away games. He wants to see me.

"To talk," he emphasizes. "How about a coffee?"

My heart spins into a frenzy. My immediate reaction is, "How dare he assume I've been sitting around waiting for his call?"

Although I sort of have.

"If you still want to talk to me," he adds.

My heart melts. "Of course, I still want to talk to you."

I'm surprised he wants to meet in public, but I go along with it. I suggest the coffee shop near my school. It's where the writers and poets meet, but there's no meeting this afternoon.

Depending on how the "talk" goes, I can head to the library and disappear into a world of books. A world that is always safe and secure when the outside world is chaotic.

Before the meeting, I rush home to take a Sangria on a walk. I cuddle him afterward to feel grounded in this new life that I am creating for myself. One that may or may not include Salvador Torres.

"Let's hope you still have a dog Dad," I whisper to Sangria before I kiss him on his furry head and leave again.

It has only been a week since the incident at the mural, but it feels like forever since I've seen Salvador's face, heard his voice, or touched his arm.

I'm anxious about what he's about to say, but I'm determined to be fully present and make wise choices.

As soon as I walk into the cafe, I see his large frame seated on a ridiculously tiny pink chair in the corner by a window.

I place my order at the counter: an espresso and one of my beloved pastries. When I try to pay, the cashier says it's already paid for.

"What do you mean?" I ask.

She indicates her head to the corner of the room, where Salvador sits looking at me. "Your boyfriend paid for it already."

My heart hitches at the word "boyfriend."

"Oh," I say. "Thank you."

I gather my tray and head toward him. His grey eyes appear luminous even from across the room. They are trained on my every step.

In my mind, I'm begging myself, "Please don't trip. Please walk smoothly without any mishaps."

I'm not a clumsy person, but with Salvador looking at me like a lion waiting for his lamb, I need to focus.

Also, it's clear as I make my way toward him that I've missed him more than I realized. I feel the smile on my face growing as I get closer to him. I want to run the last few steps but I stay cool and collected.

Salvador stands up and takes my tray, resting it on the table. He bends down to push in my chair after I'm seated, and his lips brush my hair.

An electric shock sizzles through my body at his touch. Every nerve is tingling. I yearn to throw myself at his chest, sit on his lap, put my arms around his neck, anything to be close to him.

It takes all my strength to stay in my seat and pretend that we're a normal couple having a normal conversation instead of whatever is happening here.

"Thank you for meeting me," he starts.

"Of course. How is Isabel?"

He blinks. "She misses you."

"I miss her too. Sangria misses her."

Salvador nods. "We miss him."

I don't say a word. Everybody misses everybody, now what?

"Thank you for buying my food," I say, pointing to my pastry and espresso. "The cashier said my boyfriend bought it."

A slight uptick to his lips. Finally, a hint of a smile. "I never said I was your boyfriend."

"Oh," I say a little defeated.

"Maybe she read the room right."

My breath hitches in my throat. Why would the universe send me this man who makes my life feel as if the missing piece of my heart has been found, yet make it so hard for us to be together?

That can't be right.

He leans back in his leather jacket, prominent biceps muscles bulging.

"How's school going?" I almost hear the word *sweetheart* at the end.

Okay, so we're going to avoid the topic. Or he's afraid to go there. Is it that bad?

I clear my throat. I hear my voice sound a bit too high-pitched as I tell him the details about applying for my master's degree at the university.

"And what about yourself?" I venture. "How are *you* doing?"

I want to shout, where the hell have you been? Why did you ghost me? But I'm trying hard to stay focused and calm and not let my emotions run amok.

How can you love someone and hate them at the same time? Okay, hate is a strong word. One Izzy wouldn't approve of. But *dislike*. That applies.

A large hand reaches for mine. "I'm sorry."

"For?" I retrieve my hand. Sit back, shoulders squared. My espresso has gone cold for sure. Not even my pastry looks appealing, which is saying a lot to me.

He reaches across the table again. Opens his hand and lays it palm up. Waiting for me to meet him in the middle.

"Are you okay, Corrine?"

"I'm not sure. It depends." My heart is beating faster than a fishtail out of water.

He rubs his face with his other hand as if he erasing a bad memory.

"I want to apologize again," he says, eyes full of something indescribable. Something like love?

"There are no words for the way I behaved. I'm not trying to defend being the jealous boyfriend. But I want to share with you where it comes from. I wasn't always this paranoid."

I shake my head. "It's hard to believe that you're jealous since you exude such confidence all of the time."

"I told you before it's only because of you. I've dated lots of women since breaking up . . . well since Izzy's mom left me but I never felt like this."

"Like what?" I probe.

"Like I'm going to lose you at any minute. Like someone will try to take you away. Like . . ."

"Like I'll stop loving you?"

"Yeah, that too." He creases his lips tightly. "That too."

I wonder for the hundredth time how any sane woman could leave this sweet man. And a daughter. But then there are two sides to every story. Maybe she didn't love him or them enough. Maybe she had her demons.

"Izzy's mom is Ariana Quinn. I thought you should know. No one else knows."

My mouth makes a suction cup noise.

"Ariana Quinn is your ex?"

"And Isabel's mother."

I'm going to faint. "The American singer? The actress? The celebrity? The International Diva? That Ariana Quinn?"

He nods, looking down. He slides his hand back and crosses his arms. "Yes. And the reason I wanted Izzy to learn English is I thought she should be ready for when Ariana calls. But she never does."

"Oh." I can't believe how sad that seems. My mom died, she didn't leave me and wanted nothing to do with me.

"We dated for a year. But no one knew she was pregnant. Except for me and Quinn and then my best friend, of course, not even my parents."

My immediate thought is but now I know. He's telling me this without an NDA to sign or anything.

I don't know why it's a secret, but if no one in the world knows, and now he's telling me, that means he trusts me completely.

"I won't tell anyone," I promise. I mean it, too. Not even my sisters. "It's not my secret to share. But why did you tell me."

"Because I want you to know everything." He looks at me with his gray eyes, dark and sad.

The server comes over to take our dirty dishes and sees that we're deep in conversation.

He asks quietly if we'd like anything else.

Salvador shakes his head no. I smile and say thank you, but we're fine.

The server turns to Salvador and says, "Excuse me, Mr. Torres, before you leave. Could I please get your autograph and a photo with you?"

You can tell he's worked up his nerve to ask that.

Salvador smiles at the young man. "Of course. I'll remember before I leave."

"Thank you," the server says and backs away, a large grin splitting his face.

"You're very gracious. Here you are telling me your darkest secrets and you still find it in your heart to be kind to a fan."

"My fans are everything to me," he says.

Before I can respond, he adds, "My fans are everything, but you are my life. Like Izzy."

He turns towards the window. I know it's so I don't see the sheen in his eyes.

This time it's me who places her hand in the middle of the table. I lay my palm open.

He grabs it immediately and presses it between his two hands.

"It pains me that Isabel is growing up without knowing her mother," he says softly.

"She's a monster!" I speak. "Let's call a spade a spade right now. To heck with International Divas."

A strangled laugh escapes his lips. He kisses my hand.

I hear cameras clicking around the room. I turn to my left and there are about ten photographers snapping photos and shooting videos of us sitting in the corner, talking and laughing, and trying not to cry.

"Oh my gosh, I think we're causing a scene."

"I don't care," he says. "I'll be right back."

He goes over to the camera people and shakes some hands. He signs autographs, some of them for the same writers and poets from my group who are staring at me in disbelief.

Then it looks as if Salvador is asking for privacy because he points to our table, and everyone nods and retreats.

He walks purposefully back to our table and sits down, leaning forward on his elbows.

"How long do we have?" I joke lamely.

"Well, that depends on you. I need to ask you something, Corrine. And it's not going to be easy."

Chapter Fifty-Three

He picks up my hands again but this time he slips his fingers between mine.

Oh no! Why does my heart feel like it's beating a hasty retreat right out of my body?

Maybe so it won't be blindsided by bad news.

"My proposition is . . . ."

"Wait."

I pull my hands away. Cross them on my chest, holding in anything that could burst out. It doesn't work, my mouth speaks of its own accord.

"Can you just tell me if we are done? Like whatever we *were*. Is that over?"

He doesn't say no. It's the longest silence I've ever experienced.

He ignores my outburst. "Meeting you, Corrine has given me a second chance at love. I don't want to mess it up. I don't want to lose you."

I hear the "but" coming a mile away.

"But, I'm asking you for three months."

My mind spirals. "Three months of what? We're in December. Three months will be March. What do you mean?"

I picture the calendar I started the last horrible time I heard the words, "three months."

Salvador is speaking so I halt my flashback and focus on him.

"I don't want to put you through my issues," he says. "You don't deserve that. If you can wait three months. I will dig out the man buried under triggering memories of a past relationship."

"How are you going to do that?"

"A lot of talking to the team psychiatrist. Believe it or not, football teams are recognizing that players, especially many elite players, are struggling with mental health problems. Like depression and anxiety. Even eating disorders."

I feel my eyes widen. "Eating disorders?"

"Yup," he says. "Has been an issue for several players."

"Wow! I had no idea." I'll tell him about my struggles another time. If there *is* another time.

"Anyway, the doctor suggested I find a way to focus on myself. Learn to meditate. Try different calming methods. Ways to keep myself focused on the present and manage any triggering flashbacks to the past."

"Oh."

"I will try anything. He even suggested writing in a journal. I know you do that."

"Do you think you would *like* to write in a journal? Because I don't see you doing that."

He shakes his head. "Yeah. I don't think that's happening either. We're going to have to think of something else."

"Something that makes you happy."

"You make me happy."

My heart screams, "You make me happy too," but I stay quiet.

I feel a lot of eyes on us again. I look around at the tables of customers pointing their phones at us.

I want to tell everyone to leave him alone. He's an elite footballer sure, but he's a regular human with flaws and secrets and heartbreak. And also a really good dad.

"I'm sorry about the cameras and fans," Salvador says. "It's part of the territory."

"Did I ever tell you how impressed I am at your fatherly skills? You're a great girl Dad. And a dog Dad."

He grins. "Thanks. I love being a father. And I love you, Corrine. I love you so much. I want us to be together, but I don't want to put you in any awkward situations while I fight these lingering demons."

Without realizing it, our hands are clutching each other's across the table. We're both swallowing back tears.

Three months it's not that long I say to myself. But how does he know he'll be ready to have a relationship with me or anyone in three months? It could take years.

As if he's reading my thoughts, he says, "I think you would like me a lot, Corrine when you see who I am without this dark cloak hanging over me."

"Are there any other options?" I ask in a whisper because this is going to be hard for us. It's going to be hard for me. The way I feel about him.

"I can't think of another option," he says honestly.

Part of me, the part that always tries to fix my boyfriends, wants to shout out, "I'll help."

But hasn't my travel to this new country and embracing this new life been leading me to this moment?

This is the moment when I can choose myself. Not only as a writer. Not only as a translator. But as a woman.

One who has given up bad decisions and bad boys and waiting around.

I rub his knuckles with my thumbs. I hope that he knows why I'm going to say these words to him.

"Salvador, I love you too."

"But?" he croaks out.

"I can't live my life hoping that in three months or six months or one year, you'll be ready to be in a relationship with me. I can't live my life, waiting to be chosen, waiting for the right man to be ready."

I swallow.

"What do you mean?"

"I cannot live my life for a potential you when I need to be a present me."

His voice sounds strangled. "Corrine, are you breaking up with me?

I nod slowly. Were my sisters correct that I would know what to do? Why does the right thing have to feel so awful?

"No way. You can't do that."

"I'm sorry."

He pushes the table aside as he pops up from his chair.

"I have to go," he says gruffly. "I can't believe you're throwing us away."

"I'm not throwing us away. I am choosing me."

His gray eyes penetrate my soul. "I wish you would choose *us*." Tears fill his eyes as he turns away.

He strides across the room and out the front door so fast that the people trying to take pictures of him are left dazed.

Like me.

What the hell did I do?

Was Carlos right? The hard things you must do will hurt the people you love the most.

He forgot to mention that one of those people may be *yourself.*

Chapter Fifty-Four

When I decided to stay in Portugal for the three-week holiday break because of Sangria, I knew I'd miss my family. Now it doesn't feel lonely with Daisy arriving.

"Well, that didn't go the way I imagined," Daisy says, twenty minutes after exiting the baggage claim area.

I'd wasted no time in a sympathy-seeking confession of what happened last week with Salvador.

"It didn't," I admit. "And I'm miserable. Don't ever fall in love, sis."

Daisy shimmies her shoulders as she wheels her large duffle covered with stickers of daisies. "I can't wait. I want it all. But what happened? Are you sure it isn't just a miscommunication?"

Daisy is our optimistic sister. She sees the best in everyone. A combination of Snow White and that annoying girl in *Mamma Mia* who summons all her potential fathers to her wedding.

I pull her carry-on behind me. "You have enough luggage for three months."

"I came prepared. Plus, your Christmas presents from the family are in here."

"Really?" I perk up.

"Yes, my only present is this trip. It'd better be epic."

"It will, I promise."

"As soon as we get you and Salvador sorted."

I hang my head. I don't do meek often, but Daisy brings out the humble side of me.

We head to the bus stop to catch the bus that will take us to the center of Porto.

If things had gone differently with Salvador, we'd be picking up Daisy together in one of his cars.

As we wait for the bus, I tell her more about the breakup and how torn up Salvador had seemed.

"You monster," Daisy says in mock horror. "You broke the poor guy's heart." Daisy scowls at me as she turns her face toward the bright winter sunshine.

I frown. The bus arrives and we load her luggage on board and then find two seats in the back.

Daisy shrugs out of her heavy coat. "Porto in December is like Spring in Maine," she exclaims. "This isn't a real season."

"It's lovely, isn't it?" I say subdued, proud of my new city but feeling misunderstood.

I lean back in my seat so Daisy can look out both windows.

"Don't get sensitive now," Daisy's lips curve upward. "I'm only messing with you."

I raise an eyebrow at her.

She squeezes my arm. "I can't say I understand your reasons for rejecting him."

"I'm tired of giving chances. I'm tired of fixer-uppers."

Daisy giggles. "You did date some hot works in progress. Emphasis on the 'hot.' I would love to be in your shoes. Imagine turning down a sexy football player who declared his love to you?"

"You make it sound like a fairy tale. But real life is anything but a fairy tale."

"It could be." Daisy pouts. "Just throw me your leftovers, please."

A strangled laugh escapes my throat. "Enough. Check out Porto."

I point out some landmarks as we enter the city. The Clergios Tower and the Cathedral. The Harry Potter bookstore, and the park where I met Sangria.

I don't want to be a dark cloud ruining my sister's holiday in Portugal. It's bad enough that I wake up every morning with an empty ache. Salvador Torres is no longer in my life, through my choosing.

I think about him and Isabel as the bus rolls past the colorful houses that line the Porto waterfront. I would have loved to introduce Daisy to them. They were a big part of my life here.

"You miss him, don't you?" Daisy locks eyes with me. I won't hide my feelings from my sisters anymore.

"All the time."

"Love will find its way. I'm sure of it," she says like a perky bumper sticker.

I pat her leg. "Let's hope so."

"You just have to believe."

"You'd make a great Disney princess."

She flashes a grin my way. "I'll take that as a compliment."

"You're going to find your prince one day. I mean that."

"Thanks." She goes back to staring out the window.

"Have any guys in college caught your eye? Or heart? College is full of men."

"For you. Not for someone like me." Daisy waves her hand over her curvy figure.

"But you're gorgeous." I open my phone and point to her smooth and blemish-free skin; her huge, sparkling eyes.

"And these ringlets we all would die for." I raise a handful of her twisted curls revealing strands of silvery sparkles. "What's this?"

Daisy ducks her head so I can see better. "Hair tinsel. Emerald wove them in for me."

"Ah! It's lovely. I'm glad you two have gotten past the Jackson debacle." I refer to when my two younger sisters were in love with the same boy; the high school football captain who chose Emerald over Daisy. It wrecked Daisy's heart.

"Your sparkly hair makes you look even more like a princess."

"I'd be happy for a nice sweet guy. He doesn't have to be anyone fancy, rich or royal."

"Me too," I whisper. "Me too." However, the man who has my heart is all those things. Fancy, rich, and football royalty.

Outside my apartment, Daisy marvels at the view of the bridge just like I did when I first saw this place.

"Mom would have loved it here," she says. "That view is a dream."

"I thought so too. But how do you know that? You were only seven years old when she died."

She smiles. "You forget who used to read me and Emmie fairy tales from that giant blue book every night."

"Yeah, she did that. But. . . ."

Daisy points at the gorgeous Dom Luis I bridge. "It's a replica of the illustration on the cover. Remember the title, *A Bridge to Other Lands: Fairy Tales from Around the World*."

The cover of the book. Yes! "Oh my, all this time I was wondering why I was so drawn to this bridge. Why I had to take this apartment even though it was out of my price range."

Bridge hugs me hard. "She's been here with you the whole time."

"I feel that too."

"Now can I meet my nephew please?"

After a joyous introduction, with Sangria leaping up and down and snatching Daisy's hair tie and racing around the room with it clutched in his mouth, we clip on his leash and head back out.

Our walk takes us along the waterfront and then I tell her I have a surprise for her.

"What?" she asks huffing as we start walking uphill.

"This is *Rua das flores*. The street of flowers."

"Really?" Daisy beams. "My street."

We arrive at my favorite coffee shop. I grab an empty table outside. It's chilly but with the sun shining and the heat lamps pointing our way it's quite cozy.

"This is the life, sis," Daisy remarks. "Beautiful country, handsome men, and I can't wait to try those pastries you rave about."

"The perks of a study abroad program."

"All of my sisters find true love when they travel abroad and I want to find that, too." Daisy gazes around at the window boxes of flowers on the balconies. "I've never even had a kiss or a date or anything!"

"I don't think you have to travel to find true love. Back home in Portland, we have our usual spots. We don't venture anywhere new. Maybe we should look for new spots, and explore towns we've never been to. Life can be filled with surprises even in your backyard. "

"Wow, you're waxing poetic there, Corrine."

I feel a determination to help my sister make the most of her life. The fixer part of me will never die. Maybe I should direct that energy into areas where it's actually needed.

"But I mean it, Daisy. I feel as if we live with our eyes shut going through the motions on autopilot, traveling the same roads, walking the same path, and riding our bikes on the same lanes. We're missing out. I had to travel to a new country to figure that out."

Daisy holds up her phone and pulls me next to her. "I'm taking a selfie to remember this moment with you. It's a defining moment in our lives and I want to capture it."

I smile with Daisy into the phone's camera. "Silly."

She smacks a kiss on my cheek.

"May I help you?" A deep voice asks.

I look up to find my favorite waiter. He greets me with a smile. But then turns his eyes on Daisy and his lips curve higher. I swear I see a flash of something in his eyes.

I order espressos and a couple of pastel de natas. Daisy smiles back at the waiter. She tugs at her favorite necklace, which is a chain of daisies circling her neck.

"This is my sister," I say proudly.

"May I bring you something special?" he asks her.

She blushes. "Surprise me."

His eyes, which are focused on Daisy, soften.

Daisy looks mesmerized by him, too. Her deep brown eyes are saucers. I don't blame her. He's extremely handsome. If you like them lean with sharp angles and white-blond hair, brighter than snow.

"Ahem." I interrupt their stare contest.

Daisy runs her fingers along the individual daisies on her neck.

"A woman of flowers."

She grins. "My name is Daisy."

"And mine is Leo."

"Are you from Portugal?" she asks.

"No. I'm Austrian, but I've lived in Paris for most of my life. I'm here in Porto for one year. My gap year as Americans call it."

"What are you doing on your gap year?" Daisy asks leaning closer to Leo.

His face breaks out in a massive grin. He puts up a hand to the side of his face. "I'm supposed to be learning the language and the culture. But I'm surfing!"

Daisy bursts out laughing. "I'm here for sisterly support." She glances my way. Puts her hand up to the side of her mouth. "But I'd love to learn how to surf."

Leo holds out a hand to her and they shake, while I sit back in shock.

"What?" Daisy turns to me as Leo leaves to fill our order and help other customers. "Didn't you tell me we should try new things? Walk new paths? In my case, swim new seas?"

"Yes," I say humbly. "I did. You should."

I'm happy my sister made a friend immediately. It makes me feel a bit left out though.

Which is *Wrong!* I'm free and independent and I *chose* to be this way.

My inner voice yells at me. "Shut up, Corrine. You are sad and missing Salvador too much. You really couldn't wait for the poor guy to get some help?"

I hang my head again. The third time today. And it's still early!

Chapter Fifty-Five

When we get back to my apartment, Daisy goes immediately to bed, exhausted from her long trip and our little bit of wandering about Porto.

I take out my journal and sit by the window, staring at the bridge as usual.

I've avoided my journal because I was afraid to confess my true feelings. I don't know if what I did was right or if it was a decision based on fear.

Fear of not being in control of the situation. I have no control over the timeline of Salvador's progress. No control over when he would be ready to be in a relationship. The total lack of control scares the heck out of me.

The moon above the bridge slips away in the night sky, as I fill page after page of my journal with my innermost thoughts about Salvador and how my fears maybe—*are*—inhibiting me from taking risks.

Like when we took Sangria to the animal shelter. I was afraid to keep him for plenty of reasons. It was too risky.

But Salvador, fearless and proactive, went and retrieved Sangria for me. Now I can't imagine my life without this adorable pup.

A smile sneaks across my face remembering Salvador holding up Sangria in his arms. My heart leaped with love at the sight.

So many memories of Salvador are laced with the sweetness of taking risks.

Like driving all over the Doura Valley and discovering Miguel Torga and taking on the risks of writing his story.

Even though I've never written a book in my life. Even though it would mean applying for the master's program in Portugal. Even though it would mean defying the writers and poets and creating a literary work of my own to translate.

And the kisses oh my gosh, how could I forget the feel of his body next to mine? The way he would clasp me in his arms or sit me on his knee like I was the center of his life.

How can I discard the man who challenges me to take risks? To reach higher, embrace wider, love stronger.

How could I have thrown all of that away?

I try to focus on those dark moments where he showed a side of himself that no one would like.

Even if I know the back story. It doesn't make such behavior acceptable.

The voice inside my head whispers, "He said he would work on making a change. He would conquer that dark side."

I know he will. He has the discipline of an elite athlete.

Why can't I make a change, too? Why can't I fight the fear that's holding me back?

I could stop trying to control every aspect of life and accept the things that require my patience. Instead of my calendar.

I don't know if I can do that.

I don't know *how* to do that.

But I miss him so darn much.

The truth is when the man you love says he's willing to do whatever it takes to make your relationship work, and he sets himself on that path, maybe you need to reassess your plans and make room for something magical.

Daisy is right. I don't believe in romance and magic. I don't count on it. I don't expect it.

I expect problems and loss instead.

I close my notebook and lean against the window, staring out at the bridge. How long did it take to design this architectural wonder?

How long did it take to build it?

How many people cross this bridge every day to get to the other side?

How can I cross the bridge in my heart to get to Salvador's side?

Chapter Fifty-Six

I wake up the next morning to my phone, beeping madly, and the smell of coffee brewing in the kitchen.

I check my phone to find messages from Carlos and most of my sisters asking if I'm okay.

Word must have gotten around about my and Salvador's break up. I don't respond to anyone because I don't know what to do about it.

For the first time in my life, I don't have a plan.

"What are you doing up so early?" I ask Daisy when I drag myself to the kitchen. She's wearing a cute, flowered apron with ruffles which she must have brought with her.

Sangria stands on his hind legs with his front paws on her lap as she eats breakfast.

"Don't spoil him anymore," I warn. "He's already the king of the castle."

Arf! Arf! Sangria runs over to me and leaps up and down like he's saying, "Look at me and Daisy."

I ruffle his ears. "I see you, boy."

"I slept like a hibernating bear," Daisy says.

Sangria barks at me but turns his full attention back to the sister with a plate of goodies.

"I took Sangria out for a walk."

"Thanks. Having a dog is a lot different than having a cat, huh?"

"He's adorable." She leans down and snuggles him. "I might take him with me when I leave."

"Not funny." I throw the tea towel at her. "He's my emotional support animal. I should've had one years ago."

Daisy nods with her mouth full. When she swallows, she says, "Speaking of which, sis, we are having a rom-com movie marathon tonight with the fam. For your emotional support."

"I take it you told everyone."

She nods solemnly. "Indeed. We're going to help you fix this. You look as miserable as you sound. It's called the third-act breakup."

"What?" I take a sip of coffee and frown. "What the heck did you put in this coffee? It tastes like hibiscus and something else flowery."

Daisy grins. "Love."

I pretend to gag. "How on earth do you stay cheerful and upbeat all the time?"

Part of me wonders if Mom's death affected her negatively at all.

"You mean because I am not like you guys?"

I shrug. "Kind of."

Daisy looks out the window. Twirls one of her long princess ringlets.

"I grew up watching our oldest sister Ava sacrifice her high school life to take care of everyone.

"Then I witnessed Bridget avoid emotional connections with any boy because she was scared they'd die.

"And you were planning every second of your life so you could try and control what happened. Even though you can't.

"And then there was Emerald. Her anxiety was so intense it overshadowed everything else.

"That's when I began reading a lot of fairy tales. And I refused to watch anything without a happy ever after. Still won't. I figure there is enough sadness in the world, why watch more? It may make me shallow and I know you guys think I'm superficial, but I am aware. I just choose to be happy."

I gaze at Daisy with all the love I feel in my heart. I hope she can feel it.

"It takes a very strong person to be happy when the world is a mess. It doesn't make you shallow. It makes you wise. Because I am learning we can't control the bad stuff. It happens regardless. And learning to be happy amidst the pain is a real-life skill. A survivor skill."

Daisy smiles. "I think of it that way too. I don't talk about it because it's hard being surrounded by a bunch of neurotic sisters." She laughs and sweeps her curls backward.

I smack her with the towel. "Hit a gal when she's down, why don't you?"

She laughs and gets up to put her plate in the sink. "This evening I'll introduce you to my world. The world of romance and happy-ever-afters. There's a reason it's such a popular genre. We need it."

"Well, then get dressed. We've got a full day ahead of us."

Chapter Fifty-Seven

While we get ready to go out, I text Carlos to tell him that Daisy is here and I'm taking her on a walking tour of Porto.

He texts back immediately and asks if we would like to go on his walking tour. One he has put together himself.

"What kind of tour?" I text.

"You'll see. It's not your typical Porto tour. But I think you'll like it. And it ends with a delicious snack."

"You just made that up."

He sends laughing emoji faces.

"Okay, we're coming. No need to bribe me."

Daisy and I head out with Sangria in tow.

"Can we stop at that bakery today sometime?" Daisy asks as we climb a hill to the meeting point near the iconic São Bento train station. "About three o'clock?"

"What's happening at three?" I tease, because I know exactly what, or rather who, is going to be in the bakery at three this afternoon.

She rolls her eyes at me and pulls on Sangria's leash.

"I'll tell Carlos," I assure her. "Don't worry. You'll see your prince charming again."

She giggles. "He is gorgeous, isn't he?"

Carlos is waiting for us, a fancy camera in hand. He gives Daisy a little hug and introduces himself.

When he turns around to lead the way, Daisy eyes me with an open mouth. "What a hunk!"

I smother a laugh. "Hush, he can hear you."

Carlos ignores us laughing and whispering and starts talking about Porto's street art scene.

He leads us through streets with walls covered in graffiti. Many of them are on shop fronts, some are on abandoned buildings, and some are hidden in tiny alleyways that I've never walked before.

Whole corners of buildings are adorned with giant murals that pop out at you as if they've dropped from the sky.

Daisy and I "ohh" and "ahh" as we traverse a Porto I didn't know existed.

"These works are by some of the best street artists in Portugal," Carlos explains.

"It's stunning." Daisy snaps photos of almost every single mural. "I am blown away at the colors and styles and images. How wonderful to live in an outdoor art gallery."

I nod. "I will be making these streets part of my daily walks."

"The government has been encouraging street artists and even inviting famous names to adorn the city," Carlos says.

Daisy and I tell him he must turn his street art tour into a regular event for tourists.

"People would pay to learn all this," I say.

He smiles shyly. "I am thinking of doing that. I wanted to try it out on you first. There are some tours already but I thought I'd do my own. Plus add this one."

We're standing in front of the finished mural Carlos was working on.

"Oh wow! Who did this one? It's gorgeous," Daisy exclaims.

One side of Carlos's mouth tilts up. "You want to tell her?"

"Carlos painted it."

Daisy's mouth drops open. She leaves it hanging open for a good minute. "You've got to be kidding me. You look like that and you can paint like this?"

I slap a hand over my face. "Daisy!"

"What? I'm serious."

A huge grin covers Carlos's face. "It's okay. Thank you. I am honored you like it. Your sister helped."

Daisy's eyes flash at me. "You didn't."

I point to the red flowers dotting some leaves at the edge of the mural. "I painted these," I say proudly.

Daisy walks toward the painting, her eyes narrowed. "Very nice, Corrine."

She snaps photos of my corner of the mural before stepping back and taking a lot of pictures, some with me and Carlos in them.

The memory of Salvador showing up that evening pushes its way forward.

I block it.

I will take a lesson from Daisy's book and be happy. Even if it kills me.

"This is probably the most beautiful thing I've ever seen in my life," Daisy says to Carlos.

Carlos's dark eyes twinkle and his smile brightens. "Thank you again."

"Take my picture. Take my picture." Daisy hands me her phone and runs over to pose in front of a giant tree with branches spreading over her head.

As Daisy and Carlos talk about his art, I plop down exhausted on a bench.

Sangria is wiped out from his long walk through the streets of Porto. He curls up in my lap.

He's getting way too big to be there. His tail and hind legs hang down over my lap, but he's perfectly happy and snoring away.

I pat his ears and rub my fingers through his fur.

The more I stare at the mysterious mural, with its hidden depths and lurking creatures, beautiful and regal, but a bit scary and unpredictable, the more I feel the urge to call up Salvador and blurt out, "I was wrong. I am sorry. Please forgive me."

When I call Daisy over and whisper that is what I want to do. What I *need* to do, she says no.

"You have to wait until we watch the movies tonight."

"Why?" I frown.

"Because you need a few lessons in love."

I don't argue with her.

"Let's go."

Chapter Fifty-Eight

Later, after we return from Carlos's tour with a stop at my favorite bakery where Leo greets Daisy like she's the only woman in Porto, I settle onto the sofa for my so-called romantic lessons by Netflix itself.

Although it's only two p.m. for Ava and Emerald in Portland, they're both on the couch snuggled under blankets, remote in hand.

"Is that snow outside the window?" I shout.

Emmie nods. "It's been snowing hard all day. Ava closed her store early."

Ava comes into view on the screen, handing Emerald a mug of something hot. She waves and we throw kisses back.

Bridget joins the group and we're ready to go.

"What are we gonna watch first?" Emerald asks.

I shrug. "Daisy is running the show."

Bridget raises her hand and waves it in the air. "Yes, Bridget?" we all say at the same time.

"Can we watch *51 First Dates*?"

Daisy snorts. "I am tired of telling you it's *50 First Dates*, not fifty-one."

Bridget blinks. "It should be fifty-one, because of the epic ending."

Daisy shushes her. "We are watching movies where Corrine can relate to the protagonist. Where the heroine shares her interest."

"Hmmm, they have those?" I ask skeptically.

"Netflix has every kind of romance," Emerald adds. "Jackson and I watch them all on our Netflix and chill nights."

"Those nights better be PG-rated," Ava says crossly. "And let's leave Jackson out of our girls' fest, thank you."

Emerald pouts. "I am the only sister who hasn't had boy problems."

"Whoopee." Daisy flings a finger in the air and circles it around like a victory sign for Emerald.

"I'm sorry you don't have a boyfriend yet," Emerald says.

We ignore Emmie and watch our respective screens.

Daisy selects a show that we can watch in every country. I sit back with the popcorn and a glass of sangria that we made earlier and prepare myself for a boring, overly mushy, cliché of a movie that I would never choose.

But the action gets going quickly. The movie starts with a journalist being sent undercover in a high school.

Ava claps her hands. "I love *Never Been Kissed* with Drew Barrymore."

"Ha," Emerald says. "*Never Been Kissed*. Are you trying to tell us something, Daisy?"

Daisy's face looks heated. I want to reach through the screen and throttle Emerald.

"It's one of my favorites," Bridget speaks up. "She's annoyingly smart and intellectual, just like you, Corrine. Great choice, Daisy."

Daisy relaxes against my shoulder. Sangria curls up between us.

I get wrapped up in the story of a young woman who has

never been kissed, who meets a teacher in the high school while she's on an undercover assignment.

They begin their romance over books. Shakespeare to be exact because he's a hot English teacher. I see where the fantasy part is kicking in.

"Do you like it?" Emerald squeals over the phone when the first act ends.

"I'm loving it," I say surprised.

"Keep watching," Bridget says.

I forget about clichés and find myself drawn into the drama of what it's like to fall in love for the first time and to realize that a secret is going to tear the relationship apart.

So when it happens, I shouldn't be surprised. But I am.

I'm devastated for Josie Geller.

"Stop, stop, stop. I can't watch this, it's too sad." Not to mention it's reminding me of losing Salvador.

Daisy presses pause.

My sisters groan.

"Hold on," Daisy says. She heads to the fridge and retrieves the pitcher of sangria. "I need to top up Corrine's glass."

Ava leaps up. "Gelato, Emmie?"

Emmie rubs her hands together as Ava disappears off-screen. "She made a Christmas flavor with peppermints."

Bridget stares. "I don't have any snacks!"

At that moment, we see her fiancé Ajax entering the room with a tray laden with goodies.

"Did I hear you needed snacks?" he asks, kissing her forehead.

"Were you waiting around outside the door?" she squeals.

"No," he snorts. "I know you Walker sisters. Half an hour into a call and you'll want something to eat."

I laugh at my future brother-in-law's insight into our family dynamic. I wish Salvador could meet them all. They'd love him. As much as we all love Ajax and Ava's boyfriend, Tyler.

"Can we get back to the movie?" Emerald asks, sticking her face into a large bowl of red and white gelato.

"I'm ready. I have been reinforced with another glass of sangria."

The movie plays on and I'm thinking there's no way that she's going to be able to recover from the lies.

But then Josie comes up with a plan.

"Pay attention, Corrine," Daisy urges. "This is the part for you."

I focus on the screen like my life—my love life—depends on it.

Josie has posted in her newspaper that she's never been kissed and that she's going to wait at the pitchers' mound of the big baseball game for five minutes for her one true love to come and claim his kiss.

I'm frowning. "She's gonna do what? Why?"

Every sister hisses, "*Shhhh!*"

I shake my head. "No way this will work. How is he supposed to know about the kiss on a mound thing?"

"*Shhhh!*"

I clamp my lips shut and watch.

My heart beats faster as the clock ticks down with Josie on the mound alone, exposed, and vulnerable.

Huh? This is romantic?

"Dear God. No one is showing up to kiss her. Come on. Someone in the bleachers has to find her cute and attractive. Go and kiss her, you idiots!" I shout at the screen. "Take her out of her misery!"

Daisy turns on me. "Corrine!"

I hang my head. "Sorry."

I hold my breath. And bite my tongue.

Oh my gosh, please come.

Well, I'm not going to tell you the rest. But I am panicking and sweating by the end.

"That was stressful."

"They always show up," Emerald explains. "After the grand gesture."

"The what?"

Piece by piece my sisters break down the way to win back your true love's heart. The one who messed up has to do something big to show their love.

"Oh. Do we have another movie?"

Ava, Emerald, and Bridget have to go so we say goodbye and hang up.

It's me and Daisy now. And Sangria, the pup.

"I have another one for you," Daisy says. "This one is about two sisters who can't date until the older sister, Kat, dates and Kat does not want to date so the younger sister is very upset with her."

We sit watching *Ten Things I Hate About You* in sisterly silence.

"I like Kat," I say.

Daisy rolls her eyes. "You would."

"Kat loves to read. She's applying to a wonderful East Coast college. She's a hard worker. There's nothing wrong with her."

"You're missing the point."

"Me?"

"Yes, focus on the romances."

"Okay, let's see if I got this. Older sister Kat doesn't want to date. Younger sister Bianca has two guys who want to date her. And nobody likes Kat. Is that it?"

"Yes, but there's more."

"Oh! Sexy, handsome Heath Ledger. What more do we need?"

Daisy frowns. "You are one of those horrible types who talk during movies. And yell at the screen."

"Only with rom-coms apparently," I sniff. "This movie pulls on my heartstrings even more than the last one."

"It's based on a Shakespeare play," says Daisy.

"They have modern rom-coms that do that?" I'm stunned.

"A lot of them. And on Jane Austen's books and many other classics."

"I've been missing out." I rub my hands together.

I forget to sip my sangria as I watch Kat and her suitor fall in love for real, except he's getting paid by a guy who wants to date Bianca.

They go to a party, share their private thoughts, and forge an emotional connection. I guess he feels guilty—as he should—and he doesn't kiss her when she tries to kiss him.

Granted, he's a lot cuter than she is.

She's furious and refuses to speak to him.

Heath Ledger's character can't figure out how to get Kat to forgive him until one day she's at soccer practice and he starts singing and dancing on the bleachers with a microphone and the full high school band accompanying him.

Kat bursts out laughing. All is forgiven.

For now.

"Wait until she finds out you've been paid to date her," I mutter. "No cute song and dance will save your butt then."

Daisy presses pause. "I swear, Corrine. I'll shut it off."

"Sorry, I identify with Kat."

Daisy sighs dramatically.

We watch the rest of the drama unfold in silence. Except for a few cheers and sniffs from me.

In the end, I thank my little sister. "The terrible third-act break up. I recognize it now."

"Just like you and Salvador."

"This is nothing like me and Salvador."

Daisy puts your arms around me. "You miss Salvador. You don't know how to get him back. It's the same."

"So I have to do something big, huh?"

She nods. "Huge."

"But what?"

"We'll think of something. It has to be personal to you both. Something meaningful."

I clasp my arms around my midsection.

"I could just say I'm sorry."

Daisy shakes her head. "It's too late for words."

Chapter Fifty-Nine

It turns out that I don't have to think of anything because the next morning when I wake up, I have messages from a number I don't recognize.

I slide them open one by one. They're all from the same person. Danielo.

The messages sound urgent and desperate. He writes that it has to do with Salvador and asks if I can help.

My heart wants to gallop right out of my chest.

Something has happened to Salvador? I don't bother reading the rest of the messages. I dial Danielo's number immediately.

He doesn't answer so I leave a message. It's short and frantic. "What is wrong with Salvador?"

"What do you think it's about?" Daisy asks as we walk Sangria along the river bank.

"I don't know, but I'm really worried."

We climb aboard the tram that will take us to where the river meets the Atlantic Ocean. A convergence of tides and temperaments like opposites that attract.

Her phone beeps, and she looks down and starts typing rapidly.

She misses all the sights out the window for five minutes of back-and-forth texting.

She chuckles as she dodges Sangria's wet tongue trying to swipe her face.

"It better be someone very important you're texting."

"It is," she says. "It's Leo."

"Ohhh."

Daisy yanks the bottom of her long curls and I watch as they spring up and down like an old-fashioned slinky.

I keep checking my phone to see if Danielo has texted back, but there's nothing.

I gaze at Salvador's contact information.

The numbers are like a drug tempting me to press them. I slide my phone into my pocket and focus on the surroundings. Be present, I remind myself.

We get off at the last stop and walk towards the beach.

Many folks are out enjoying the early winter sunshine.

On the semi-crowded promenade, Sangria stops and starts to smell every clump of grass.

It gives me a chance to check my phone.

Needless to say, we make slow progress on our walk.

"This is beautiful," Daisy says. "It reminds me of home. Windswept beaches, lighthouses, rocky pools of seawater."

"Except Porto has an international surf culture. All kinds of water sports."

"Yes, Leo has been telling me about it."

"You're not really thinking of trying to surf are you?"

"Why not?" she shrugs. "Anything is possible."

I frown. "Better not tell Dad."

She laughs at me. "I am eighteen, almost nineteen. I can surf if I want to."

"Now you sound like my baby sister again."

Even though it's December, people are sitting on the rocks in the sun.

We've walked quite a ways until we get to a section of the beach that is filled with surfers and kite borders.

Their families and friends are spread out on blankets watching their loved ones challenge the waves.

We plop down on the sand in our jeans and yoga pants. I pull out my water bottle and pour some out into Sangria's portable bowl. He laps it up and looks to me for more.

An hour later, the breeze picks up and I start gathering our stuff to leave.

"This is the perfect combination of fun and relaxation, isn't it?" I tickle Sangria under his chin. "But we must go now."

Arf! he agrees.

"I could see you living here," Daisy says, standing up.

"You could?"

"Couldn't you? I think that if you could stay here and do your master's degree here, you should. Porto lights you up. You've never looked this relaxed back home. And I haven't even met Salvador yet."

She's right. I've never felt this relaxed. Even with the sadness of missing Salvador.

"I think it's because when I was home I felt surrounded by sadness all the time. I was constantly managing the amount of sadness I would let into my life. But here, I have a fresh start."

"That's what I see."

"They say if traveling doesn't change you then you're not doing it right."

My phone suddenly starts beeping loudly and I grab it out of my bag. It's Danielo calling.

My heart beats a thousand drums.

"Corrine," he starts. "It's me, Danielo. We need your help."

At that moment, Leo appears, sleek in a wetsuit, with a surfboard balanced on his head. He's walking across the sand toward us. Daisy runs across the sand to him.

I swear they greet each other like long-lost lovers.

I turn all my attention back to my dire romantic issues.

"How can I help?" I ask.

Chapter Sixty

Danielo's news is harsh. I haven't been following the football games on television or online because they are a painful reminder of my and Salvador's failed relationship.

But now I'm hearing Danielo tell me that Salvador's been too depressed to play.

"Corrine," Danielo wails in a voice unexpected for a pro athlete. "We're in the championship league now. One of our biggest games is going to be in Porto next weekend. We have to win to stay in the league."

"You'll be playing at home?" Is that joy flooding my heart?

"But Salvador won't be in the game. He's suffering badly. His mental health is affecting his performance."

"Suffering?" My mood ricochets from joy to fear.

"YES!" Danielo shouts at me as if I'm not registering his urgency. "He misses YOU!"

"Oh."

"Because you broke up with him. He's having a hard time. He says it's all his fault because he acted like an idiot for being so jealous of your friend. He told me the whole story. I've never seen

Salvador let personal issues affect his game. This is different. YOU are different."

"What can I do to help?"

I'm more concerned for Salvador than I am for the team.

"I'm not saying to take him back. I'm not saying to do anything you don't want to do. But can you please come to the game? It's Saturday and I will leave tickets for you to be in seats right next to the field. I think it would mean a lot to him. And the team. We need our star player back."

"Are you going to tell him I'm coming?"

"No." I can almost see Danialo shaking his head. "We want him to see you there. We think that will inspire him to play."

The wheels are turning in my head. This could be my chance to create a grand gesture.

"I will come. I do have a request."

I glance over at Daisy smiling with a face of sunshine and happiness and Leo with his white-blond hair blinding me.

"May I have a few more tickets? Is that possible?" I ask.

"Of course. You can have six tickets. You can have eight tickets."

"Five is fine," I say. I've already counted them out in my head.

One for Daisy, one for Leo. One for me. One for Sylvia, and one for Sylvia's friend Frank. Because I am not doing this alone.

Inviting Carlos may cause the entire plan to backfire. Carlos likes me for more than a friend. Salvador was right. Even if the feeling isn't being reciprocated. I don't need to show up at Salvador's football game with another man.

"Text me the time and where to pick up the tickets and we will see you next Saturday. And Danielo, please keep him safe."

Danielo thanks me. "Is there any chance of you two getting back together?" he asks hesitantly. "He loves you like he's never loved anyone else."

"I miss him. So very very much. I even miss his annoying, overconfident, macho bits."

Danielo laughs and says he'll be rooting for us.

After I hung up, I realized it was all true.

I miss Salvador's energy. His way of challenging me to think big. His committed love. His larger-than-life presence. And the way he cups my head to kiss me like I am the most precious thing in the world.

I miss that most of all.

Chapter Sixty-One

Saturday morning arrives full of sunshine dazzling off the Dom Luís I bridge.

"What are you gonna wear?" Daisy asks. "And more importantly, what is your master plan? Your grand gesture to win back your man?"

I glance down at my outfit of leggings, short boots, a long sweater, and my leather jacket. "What's wrong with what I'm wearing?"

"What's *wrong* with what you're wearing? It's what you always wear!"

"And?"

"You're going on an epic journey. Do you understand we're going to an arena where your man is competing in physical combat and you're his lady? The person who holds his heart in her hand."

I scoff at my sister. "What's happening here is he's doing his job and I am going to be supportive."

She blinks hard.

"And try to win him back," I add meekly.

"Corrine. This is a once-in-a-lifetime moment. Today will decide your and Salvador's fate. You must dress accordingly."

"Like what?"

She puts a finger to her lips. "Uhm . . . like Bridget Jones when she had to declare her love to Mr. Darcy and put on her prettiest dress. Although it got soaked."

"I didn't read that."

"Or . . . Josie Geller. She was wearing that pretty floral dress, right?"

"She was. Impractical for a baseball game."

I head back to my room. "I was already nervous, but now . . . I don't have the right clothes!"

She follows me, reaching inside my closet and pushing hangers aside, searching for God knows what.

"Why are all your clothes black?" she asks.

"Because that's my signature color."

"We need a new signature color for the new you. Enough with this pseudo-intellectual look."

"Have you been talking to Salvador?" I demand.

"No, but I can't wait to."

"Anyway, you're wasting your time. I have nothing that would fulfill your romantic notions of what's happening today."

She puts her hands on her curvy hips and surveys me up and down. "Don't you want to make an impression on him? Show him you've changed your mind. That you love him. That you're *in* love with him."

"Of course, you know I do. Showing up at his football game and showing my support is my grand gesture."

"You don't go to your grand gesture looking any old way. Everybody knows that."

I slide down on the bedspread. "Okay, show me the way, master. I can't believe I'm letting you choose what I'll wear to a football game. To see a man. By the way, make sure it's not the other team's colors."

"I'm pretty sure the other team's colors won't be floral."

I grab my head. "Flowers?"

Daisy nods. "Flower power, baby. But we don't have time to go shopping. And none of my clothes will fit you."

"Come with me." I yank her by the wrist. "We're going to Sylvia's."

Chapter Sixty-Two

Sylvia proves to be my fairy godmother once again.

While she shows us her closet, her hot guitarist boyfriend Frank stirs a pitcher of sangria in the kitchen.

The funny thing with Frank is his accent is a combination of Australian and Portuguese because he spent so much time down under playing in a band.

"Do you young women want a glass of freshly made sangria?" His dark eyes crinkle with his warm smile.

We tell him we will drink later. After the wardrobe debacle is resolved.

Sylvia kisses his cheek. "We have work to do, darling. Keep the sangria cold and sweet. We'll be back."

I tell her about the grand gesture as Daisy surveys the closet bulging with clothes of every fabric. Her eyes are wide and she looks like she's in a toy shop.

"That's wonderful," Sylvia gushes. "I think Salvador is the right man for you. He challenges you but also adds fun to your studious nature."

"I think so, too. I'm glad that you met somebody to share your life with."

"It only took us forty years to get it right."

"You've waited forty years for him? He seems like a great guy, but wow, that's a long time."

Sylvia's laugh tinkles across the room. "I didn't sit on my hands and twiddle my thumbs, as the saying goes. I had a full life. But honestly, when you know you know. And I knew that Frank was the one for me when I was nineteen years old."

Daisy nods. "I believe that."

"I do, too. Salvador is the one for me. Even if it has taken me a while to believe it."

"Well honey, the important thing is you realized it. Now stand still."

I stand like a doll as Sylvia and Daisy hold up beautiful dresses and pant suits against my frame before choosing a few for me to try on.

I head into the bathroom with a pantsuit that I love, a silk wraparound dress, and a flirty flowery dress with material so light it feels like fairy wings when I spin around.

"What the heck is this, Sylvia?" I step out of the bathroom, tiptoeing in the last one. "I look like a ballerina."

"I bought it for a special occasion."

"What occasion was that?" I pry. "Looks like you never wore it. The price tag is still on."

"A date with a young man."

Daisy and I exchange looks.

Sylvia sighs, "If you must know, I bought it forty years ago to find Frank and declare my love for him. I was planning on telling him I'd go with him to Australia. But he'd already left because of our argument."

"This was your grand gesture dress?" I ask in shock. "I can't wear it."

"Why not? I don't need it anymore," Sylvia cackles. "He's right out there."

"As long as you don't need it today," Daisy adds. "This is the perfect dress."

"You look stunning. Stylish but sweet." Sylvia agrees.

"Sweet? I want the 'girlfriend of an elite footballer' look. This is more of a 'take a chance on me,' look, I could be a mythical creature."

Daisy and Sylvia burst out laughing.

"Corrine, this dress was made for you. I did not imagine meeting a young woman perfect for it. One who would be like a daughter to me. But I'm so glad I have." Sylvia wipes her eyes.

I rush to her side. "And you are like a mother to me."

I don't complain anymore. This is the dress.

If it's my mother who imprinted the image of the Dom Luís I bridge in my soul as a child, and if that bridge is the reason I moved to this building, then it's my mom who has brought Sylvia and me together.

And this dress is for me. A gift from my earthly mother.

No way I can lose today.

Chapter Sixty-Three

The stadium is teeming with people making their way in, tickets held high.

I get our tickets and hand them out to each person.

Sylvia and Frank came with me and Daisy. Leo was outside waiting for us. After I introduce everyone to each other, we make our way inside.

Everywhere I look, I see vendors selling football gear, t-shirts, hats, scarves, everything with Porto FC on it.

I head over to one of the vendors and I ask if they have Salvador's t-shirt with his number 32.

I'm told it is one of the most popular jerseys, so I have to try five vendors before I find one.

I toss it over my dress and leather jacket. It hangs to my knees.

"Well guys, what do you think?" I ask approaching my group.

Daisy is laughing her head off. Sylvia shakes her head. "All our hard work is wiped out."

Frank gives me a thumbs-up.

Leo's eyes are wide. "It's *the* Salvador Torres you're in love with?"

"He's in love with her, too." Daisy pats Leo's arm.

Leo whips off his belt and comes over to me. "Here. Put this on. It will make the jersey a lot cuter."

Daisy grins. "Thank you, Leo. Please lend us a little Parisian fashion sense."

I hold up the belt to Leo. "Be my guest."

By the time Leo is done, everyone says I look great. Leo has managed to belt the oversized jersey in a way that my flirty skirt still flutters around my legs.

Our seats are amazing. We might as well be in the game we're so close to the field.

I focus my mind on being fully present in this moment and tell myself the result is not as important as the message I need to communicate to him. But who am I fooling?

Right before the game starts, the players step onto the field. Salvador stands right next to our seats. I feel as if I've been knocked over by a powerful wave.

"Corrine," Daisy pokes me. "Wave your hand so he can see you."

But I'm frozen.

My legs shake, but not from the chilly air.

It's him. Standing there. Powerful. Unflinching. His eyes roam the stands as if he can feel me here.

Then he finds me.

His eyes lock on mine.

If I wasn't sitting down, I'd collapse.

The strength I was harvesting from those around me seeps away.

It's only me. It's only Salvador.

No one else. An entire stadium of fans fades away as he strides toward me.

We are literally on *his* turf.

Daisy's cold hand squeezes mine but I don't feel a thing.

Every cell in my body is on fire as the man I love with all my heart steps in front of me.

I'm trembling as I slip out of my coat. I want him to see the jersey I'm wearing. I want it to be clear.

"I am here for you."

His eyebrows twist up as if doubting my words.

He glances at his team.

This may be my only chance to speak.

"I know you have an important game to play. I came because I love you. I miss you. I want you in my life. I am so sorry for not believing in us."

I'm talking very fast. My words are tumbling over each other because I have no time to waste.

The pressure is immense. I feel as if I am on speakerphone to an entire stadium of people and if I don't hurry up, they're going to start shouting and booing me for distracting the star player.

"Did you hear me? Did you hear what I said?" I ask in a strained voice.

He's showing no reaction.

Finally, he nods his head. "Thank you for coming." His voice is formal and polite.

His eyes reveal nothing as if we've never had a connection at all. My heart sinks straight to my feet. I reach out my hand to touch his and he moves his hand away.

"I have to go. I hope you guys enjoy the game." He gives a little wave to everyone near me.

"Wait, please," I say.

He stops for a second and turns, "I did wait. It's you that couldn't."

Then he turns and runs off onto the field.

I have no idea what happens in the game.

Salvador is a blur running up and down the field, scoring goals, faking the ball away from rival players, and playing one of the best games of his life, according to the announcers.

Danielo raises a thumbs up to me. I can't tell him I didn't fix anything.

Salvador is performing as the athlete he's trained to be. He doesn't need my help at all. He's winning for his hometown fans. He won't let them down.

And it's clear I no longer mean anything to him.

A deep anguish spirals through me.

Daisy puts her arm around me on one side. Sylvia on the other.

All I can think is I must find a way to live with this loss.

Chapter Sixty-Four

It's one week before Christmas and Daisy and I have decorated my apartment from top to bottom with beautiful tinsel and garlands of flowers that we found in the central market.

I'm not feeling cheery but I rally for Daisy. And Sangria.

Sylvia comes over every day with homemade Portuguese casseroles and the bread she bakes with Frank.

My classes are finished and so are all the papers I had to turn in.

I feel good about this semester despite everything that's happened. I've learned a lot, not just from books, not just about what I can do with my language skills, but I've learned about myself.

Dad calls me one morning to talk to me about how I'm feeling. His familiar dark eyes smile back at me crinkling up in the corners. The gray at his temples is more pronounced.

"I heard you and Maxine broke up," I venture. I don't say, "Like me and Salvador."

"Yes. Breakups happen. But when it is with the person you are meant to be with, you mend it. You do whatever it takes."

"Is Maxine the right person for you?"

He shakes his head. "Sadly, no. I had the right person once. And we did break up early in the relationship."

"What? You and Mom broke up?"

He tells me a story about the first time he and my mom fought. It was a story I had not heard before, and I knew he was telling it to me to help me right now.

"We'd been dating for one year. But we broke up. For five months. It was terrible."

"Why? What happened?"

"It doesn't matter what the argument was about. Which is what I figured out. The important thing was how to mend the relationship."

"Are you gonna tell me how? Or are you gonna make me wait?" I joke because he's staring in the distance behind my shoulder like mom is there saying, "Tell the story right."

"The thing is," Dad starts again, "Your mom was wrong. She claimed to have seen something a certain way that didn't happen at all.

"I wrote her a few letters explaining that what she thought she saw, she didn't see. Because it didn't happen. She was wrong. But she didn't respond."

"Oh no," I feel sad for the young man my father was, trying to fix a misunderstanding.

"I tried to talk to her in person, and she kept insisting that the events had occurred exactly the way she remembered them."

"So what did you do?" I ask, intrigued with how my parents got past this dilemma.

"I told her she was right."

"What?" I'm flabbergasted. "You told her she was right even though you knew she was wrong?"

"Yes, I did. I loved her and I missed her. The breakup was not going to be resolved unless I pivoted. So I did. I told her she was right."

"Wow. I didn't know mom was stubborn like that."

"Oh yes, my dear. I don't dwell on her flaws, but her flaws

made her just right for me. Don't be afraid of the flaws in the person you love. As long as they don't harm you. Be open and accepting and above all, try to love them. I grew to love your mother's stubbornness. I would even tease her about it."

I laugh. "Thanks for telling me that story, Dad. But didn't you feel you were compromising your belief in the truth?"

"Nope. She would never admit that she was wrong. She never saw it from my point of view. I had to suck up my pride and go for the girl I loved. I'd do it again."

"I'm glad you did."

"You know that saying, 'It's better to be happy than right'?"

I chuckle. "Yes."

"It's true."

"Thank you, Dad, for the advice."

When we hang up, I head outside to walk Sangria. Daisy is off on a date with Leo.

I walk strong and fast as little Sangria's legs skip alongside me.

"Hey boy," I talk to Sangria. "I said I was wrong. I apologized. The ball is in his court. Ball, ha!"

Sangria tilts his head at me. As if to say, "You need to try harder."

As I turn back toward home, I think about Dad's words. The deeper meaning. It's about not getting caught up in waiting for the other party to come to his or her senses. Or whose court the ball is in.

It's about seizing the day.

We turn the corner and I see the car that I know so well. The little red sports car is parked at the curb, but there's no one in it.

My heart almost gallops right out of my chest.

"Hold on, Sangria," I say pulling in his leash. It seems he recognizes Salvador's car too. Or his scent.

I look around. Is he near here?

I keep walking. Maybe he's in the cafe nearby.

After a half mile of walking and gazing around, I tell Sangria it's time to head home.

I can't help but sigh at the irony of the situation.

A few months ago I walked around Porto, hoping I would not run into Salvador Torres.

Now, I'm walking around Porto, hoping I do.

Chapter Sixty-Five

After a wonderfully small but intimate Christmas dinner at Sylvia and Frank's place, Daisy and I take a short flight to Paris to hang out with Leo for the week between Christmas and New Year's Eve.

He has a surprisingly large apartment for a gap-year student and a seemingly bottomless wallet as he takes us on a whirlwind tour of the City of Lights.

I like Paris, but not as much as I love Porto.

Daisy is enamored. I'm not sure which she loves more, Paris or Leo.

We don't meet Leo's family, which is a bit strange, but I don't ask why. Families and holidays don't always match up.

On New Year's Eve, we head back to Porto.

"I heard that Sangria Nights is having a big New Year's Eve party," Sylvia says as we enter her apartment to collect Sangria. "Maybe you girls can go check it out."

"I don't know," I shake my head. "I can't handle seeing Salvador tonight. Plus, I missed Sangria."

He's leaping at my feet and barking excitedly. I stoop down to pick him up.

"I missed my baby." I press kisses all over his furry head.

"He can spend one more night with me and Frank," Sylvia says, "He's family."

"I heard there was a live band there," Franks adds. "A good one."

"Sounds like we should go. Come on." Daisy pulls me inside. "We're going to change clothes then head out. Love you guys, Happy New Year."

Sylvia opens her arms. "Put Sangria here and go get ready. I left a sparkly dress on your bed. It's a night of new beginnings."

"Thanks, Sylvia." I hug her and kiss Sangria one more time.

"What's going on?" I ask suspiciously as Daisy changes fast into a cute party dress with boots and touches up her makeup. "You're acting a little weird."

She shakes her head. "Nothing. I'm excited to see Leo again."

"We just saw him twenty minutes ago. For a week!"

She waves her hand in the air. "We are going out to celebrate life. Is that better?"

I eye her closely. I know my sister well. She's acting a bit manic.

As I slip on Sylvia's gorgeous dress, I assess how I feel about going to Salvador's bar.

Whatever feelings I have for Salvador, I'll be living in Porto. I'll see him. I certainly will hear about him.

So, the sooner I cross over into his territory, the better for me.

When we arrive at Sangria Nights, the place is a madhouse of loud fun.

Live music plays inside, with people dancing and blowing on noise makers.

Outside a DJ plays in a decorated hut. Heaters warm up the chilly air.

Waiters sporting golden New Year's crowns walk around with pitchers of red and white sangria, filling glasses with the frothy fruit drink.

If Salvador is here, I wouldn't even see him.

He's not going to notice me either. Not with the crowd of partygoers streaming inside and out.

Daisy and I head out to the patio area. We can see the whole bridge. It's lit up with thousands of blinking white lights.

"I love this city," I tell Daisy. " I could live here forever."

"You do look happy here, as I've said a hundred times. Just accept it. Even without a boyfriend, Porto is your place."

"It sure is." I twirl around, raising my glass high. "Here's to Porto!"

"To Porto!" Leo chimes in, walking up with Carlos by his side. "Look who I found."

"You guys know each other?" I ask.

"Porto is not that big," Leo says. "Daisy showed me photos of his mural and photos of all you guys in front of it. I have to see it in person."

Carlos raises his glass. "To Porto."

I look at my sister-friend group and feel like I *am* ready for new beginnings.

At the countdown to midnight, Leo, Daisy, Carlos, and I are laughing and chatting with some university students. We're all raising our glasses because the DJ has told us to.

And then the countdown begins.

Five, four, three, two, one.

I get hit with a dollop of sadness at the moment I say "one" knowing that if things had gone differently, I'd be kissing Salvador Happy New Year right now.

An explosion of gold, red, and purple lights fills the sky as fireworks explode around Porto.

The bridge drips silvery stars from its topmost level.

"Oh my, look at my life," I whisper to myself.

Daisy is going around saying cheers and clinking glasses with everyone in her radius.

Leo watches her with a loving smile on his face. I'm blessed to see my baby sister find a guy who adores her the way she deserves.

At that moment the DJ stops the music. He calls for everyone to be quiet.

"Ladies and gentlemen, may I have your attention, please? Happy New Year to you all, but I need your attention."

Almost everyone gets quiet. We turn to the DJ.

"I have a special dedication."

A hush goes up.

"This song is dedicated to Miss Corrine Walker."

I gasp.

Daisy rushes over to my side a big smile on her face. "It's for you."

I don't know what's happening.

Then I hear the song I love.

The one that reminds me of my mother, who died of cancer when I was eleven years old. It was later I learned that the songwriter/singer composed it for his own mother, who also died of cancer.

The words and the music could not be more beautiful.

Drops of Jupiter by Train plays over the speakers. I'm choking up so much I can hardly breathe.

It has to be Salvador who requested this song for me because he's the only one I told about it.

That means he's here. I turn around to look for him. I need him. Not just now. I need him forever.

And there he is. Standing before me with a look of pure love on his face.

His eyes soften. "I thought I could live without you. But you are the blood running through my veins. Only a fool would turn his back on this kind of love. I am sorry I was a fool."

"I'm sorry too." Like Dad said, it doesn't matter who's right and who's wrong. Or whose turn it is to apologize. The important thing is to say you're sorry. And be with the one meant for you.

Tears gather in my eyes and I blink hard. I don't want to miss a moment of what's happening right now. I want to remember this forever.

Salvador takes me in his arms and we sway side to side singing the beautiful lyrics to each other.

"You played my song," I whisper into his ear.

"I had to get your attention, my love. This song was the only way I knew how. I want to be the reason that you never want to leave this earth. I want to be your everything the way you are mine."

I reach up to kiss him and wrap my arms around his neck.

"You are everything I've always wanted." I lean back to look deeply into his eyes. "All of the sorrows and pain I endured have led me to this moment with you."

He brushes my hair off my face and kisses my forehead. "You said you didn't want to wait . . . "

I interrupt him. "I shouldn't have said that."

"Hush, it's okay. It made me realize we don't have to wait apart. Whatever we have to work on, we're going to do it together. We're never leaving each other again. I promise you if you can promise me the same."

I don't trust myself to speak. I nod my head.

"I have something else for you," he says.

I can barely see because the tears are falling down my face. Tears of happiness.

Salvador points out at the river toward the bridge.

People are gasping, some are clapping.

I squint to see what it is they're looking at.

From on top of the Dom Luís I, a scroll of golden threads has unfolded. It falls halfway down almost to the water. It's waving in the breeze, but I can see the words.

Will you marry me, Corrine?

My hand goes to my throat.

Salvador's breath tickles my ear. "I love you, baby. I want to start a new beginning with you."

I have no words. Me, the woman of words, is speechless.

Daisy grips one of my arms. Her eyes are shining, but she doesn't look surprised.

"You already knew about this?"

"Yes," she squeals. "All of us knew."

Salvador's arms are around me from behind. He's holding me so close to him I can hear his heart beating.

His chin rests on top of my head. I know that I am 100% safe as long as I stay right here with him for the rest of my life.

"Well?" he asks. "Are you going to make me wait again?"

I choke out a sob. "Never. Yes, I love you. Yes, I will marry you."

Salvador shouts. "She said yes!"

The entire patio rings out with shouts of congratulations.

The DJ puts on Bruno Mars *Marry You* song and everyone starts dancing in the cold night air.

It's the perfect night and I'm with the man who's not perfect, but who is perfect for me.

"I have to call my family," I shout.

Daisy holds up her phone. "Don't worry. They were part of it, too."

"Even Dad?" I ask.

Daisy nods. "Him too."

I hear my sisters shouting over the phone, "Where's the ring?"

Salvador says, "Hold on."

He calls Danielo over. "My best friend has the ring. Sorry, I was so excited I forgot that part."

"Me too," Danielo apologizes. He hands Salvador a beautiful blue box.

And then Salvador gets down on one knee. My big football hero, in front of my dad and my sisters on a video call, in front of his entire restaurant and bar and half the people in Porto, and says, "One more time, Corrine Walker, will you marry me?"

I put a finger to my lip and pretend to think about it.

Salvador doesn't wait for my answer. He grabs my hand and slips the ring on.

"Too late, you already said yes."

I shake my head at my future husband. "A woman can change her mind."

"Not *my* woman," he says. "Champagne for everyone," he shouts above the music.

"You mean no sangria?"

"No, baby. Tonight it's all champagne."

We drink the sweet bubbly wine and share cold kisses under Porto's winter sky.

The old year is ending and the new one is starting just as they should.

With promises of new beginnings.

"I can't wait to tell Izzy and Sangria," I say to Salvador.

"Can you imagine the chaos to come?"

I smack my forehead. "I'll need a new journal."

We both laugh, not because it is funny, but because we will find our way.

♥ Dear Reader,

Please <u>Leave a Review</u> on Amazon to help others find this book! It can be as short as you want! It would mean a lot to me as an indie author. Thank you.

♥ If you enjoy the Walker sister romances, Daisy's and Leo's story is next in Paris Forever!

About the Author

Lynn Joseph is from Trinidad & Tobago. When she's not writing her international romances, she can be found on a beach somewhere in the world. Or binge-watching *Hart of Dixie* and *The Vampire Diaries* over and over. Lynn lives in charming South Portland, Maine, and on the Caribbean Island of Tobago, where she's known as the Mermaid Queen. Join her on her journey of love, food, and romantic destinations (not necessarily in that order). www.lynnjosephbooks.com

Stay Connected

Sign up for Lynn's newsletter and receive a FREE ebook, *Princess Aboard*. Plus be in the know for all the behind the scenes goodies and more!

Sign Up Here —>
https://BookHip.com/NKSQGRS

Follow her on social media:

Facebook -http://facebook.com/lynnjosephauthor
Instagram - https://www.instagram.com/lynnjosephbooks/
Bookbub - https://bit.ly/3Phcsuu
Amazon - https://amzn.to/3VTd8Kb
Goodreads -https://bit.ly/4gUtZo4

Lynn loves to hear from her readers and invites them to email her, anytime at lynn@lynnjosephbooks.com

www.lynnjosephbooks.com

Also by Lynn Joseph

The Walker Sisters Forever Series

(Sweet Romance)

Gelato Forever

Olives Forever

Sangria Forever

Paris Forever

Christmas Forever

Cocoa Reef Resort Series

(Steamy Romance)

Lime to My Coconut

Rum to the Reggae

Spice for My Santa

Princess Abroad

(Read for FREE! —> https://BookHip.com/NKSQGRS)

9 7 9 8 9 8 8 0 4 8 6 5 7